PATRICE CHAPLIN is author and playwright two dozen books. Her *Albany Park*, *Siesta* (whi

ring Jodi Foster and Isabella Rossellini), *Into the Darkness Laughing*, *Hidden Star*, *Night Fishing* and *Death Trap*. Her stage play *From the Balcony* was commissioned by London's National Theatre in conjunction with Radio 3. As a Bohemian in Paris during the 50s and 60s, Patrice spent time with Jean Paul Sartre and Simone de Beauvoir. Married to Charlie Chaplin's son, Michael, and living and working in Hollywood, she was friends with everyone from Lauren Bacall and Miles Davis, to Salvador Dali and Jean Cocteau, who gave her a starring role in one of his films.

In her books *City of Secrets* (2007), *The Portal* (2010) and *The Stone Cradle* (2017) Patrice opened the door to entirely new and compelling elements of the Rennes-le-Château mystery involving the mysterious Catalan capital of Girona. She continues the discovery of hidden secrets in *The Unknown Pursuit*.

Patrice is the director of The Bridge, a non-profit organization that leads workshops based in the performing arts as a new and unique way to help fight addiction. She lives in North London.

THE UNKNOWN PURSUIT

THREE GRANDMOTHERS
IN SEARCH OF THE GRAIL

A TRUE STORY

PATRICE CHAPLIN

CLAIRVIEW

Clairview Books Ltd.,
Russet, Sandy Lane,
West Hoathly,
W. Sussex RH19 4QQ

www.clairviewbooks.com

Published in Great Britain in 2019 by Clairview Books

A CIP catalogue record for this book is available from the British Library

ISBN 978 1 912992 06 5

Cover by Morgan Creative featuring Girona Street Scene © Santi Rodrigues
Typeset by DP Photosetting, Neath, West Glamorgan
Printed and bound by 4Edge Ltd., Essex

This is a true story that happened as written and only the names of individuals have been changed to protect their identities.

Three women arrive in Girona, North East Spain, to attend a new-age metaphysical workshop based on the mysteries of this ancient city. They have never met. What do they have in common? They find they are all grandmothers. They know little about metaphysical or psychic dimensions. What do they want? To keep a good face on things. Things being quite a lot of difficult issues. What do they really want? Life change? Reclaiming their dreams? What do they actually get? The Holy Grail. And all they were looking for was a way out of sudden old age.

Chapter 1

Lady Cynthia Seymour-Coy and Mia Zang took the same cheap flight from London to Girona, North East Spain. Mia did notice Cynthia's ebullient mass of blonde hair as she was moved to a preferential seat and Mia with her lacklustre appearance was kept back in steerage. The bright hair helped by a little bleach looked young and had been that way, Mia decided, since the woman had had her first conquest. It had worked then. Why change it? She generated good nature and a desire for the best outcomes.

Later in the passport queue they, two English women of a certain age travelling alone, started speaking. Cynthia had a smart voice, confident and crisp and had been to the right schools. She was going to join a metaphysical group in Girona. She didn't know much about it except treatments were included at an old-fashioned spa somewhere in the countryside and this appealed to her. 'Mud and sulphur water, that sort of thing.' She was desperately tired and hoped there would not be too much physical activity and no obligatory diet. There had been mention of some advanced yoga, a pilgrimage and sightseeing which seemed to include climbing a mountain. She would stick to what the spa had to offer. Mia supposed this was the well-known Balneari Prats at Caldes de Malavella, a wonderful family-run establishment that had survived decades and had no need to change. Cynthia generously suggested Mia join her and try it out. 'The group leader who runs it gives talks on other dimensions. She's well known on that subject.' Cynthia couldn't remember her name.

Mia had brought her painting equipment and as she had little money, perhaps she could give one or two art classes in exchange for payment.

'Transformation,' said Cynthia. 'That's what it's about. You come out supercharged.'

For Mia this was too Hollywood. She'd heard it a hundred times. But she liked Cynthia and found her comforting. A group? She'd join it. At least she'd have somewhere to stay while she revisited whatever it was in that city that could kick start her life.

She helped Cynthia with her outsize luggage and spoke enough Spanish to get them to the hotel, located in the town centre, by the river. The eighteenth century building had once housed ecclesiastical students. In front of the entrance a wide pedestrian passageway with shops and bars on both sides and public benches placed in a row down the middle, offering at one end, shadow, the other sun. Mia suggested a walk and Cynthia would be delighted but first she had to let her husband know she had arrived. 'He always wants to know exactly what I'm doing. You know how husbands are.'

Mia did. But not that kind of husband.

The clanking iron bridge crossing the main river marked the place where the modern town met the old quarter. The atmosphere was light, lively and meaningful. Good things had happened in this place. It was early spring and for the first time in a long while Mia felt optimistic. Several old bridges crossed the narrow river which curved through the centre of town and the buildings on both sides were centuries old and colourful. The huge cathedral rose above it all and church bells across the town joined its sonorous rich chime and rang out the new hour. Yes, it was as Mia remembered. The iron bridge designed by Eiffel was unchanged and swayed a little in the wind. Even the essences in this wind from the south had survived the passing of time and she thought she could still smell the toilet water the men put in their hair, wood smoke, and anis liquor.

Cynthia was impressed and her spirits rose further as she sat at one of the many outside bars and sampled a glass of local wine. Mia remembered the light pink innocent drink that kept her dancing through till dawn. 'It comes from Perelada, a village near here. This is a young wine.' They had another and then two more and they even started to feel young.

'You've been here before,' said Cynthia.

'Just passing through.' Mia ordered local toasted bread smeared with tomato, oil and garlic, topped with strips of the finest Iberian ham. Now was the moment to put their best cards on the table. Mia introduced herself as the painter Mia Zang and implied she was well

3

known in the States. She was here to find a fresh direction to her work for the forthcoming show in LA. Cynthia assured her she knew her name. In return, to match this outbreak of fame she, Lady Cynthia-Coy, brought forward the husband who now had the presence and danger of a Marlon Brando.

'I am crazy to leave him on his own. Women will do anything. I have to keep awake around him. Maybe that's why I'm so tired.' And now as well as women he suddenly collected art. She said, 'Let's send him a sample of your work. He likes the real things.' Cynthia realized to talk like this meant she had careened away from any known reality and must be a little tipsy. Art collector? Him? She decided it was time to go to the hotel and lie down.

One or two people sitting in the foyer looked up expectantly. 'Are you for the group?' And a French elfin in a green silk dress belonging to another age, possibly the 1950s, came forward to greet them. Her tiny deeply tanned face was wizened, her eyes, as green as the dress, darted inquisitively from Mia to Cynthia. The eyes didn't miss much. Mia thought she had been a performer.

Cynthia agreed she was 'for the group'.

'Kelly hasn't got here yet.' The woman's tone was deep and smoky. 'You've not seen her?'

Cynthia not knowing who she meant supposed she hadn't.

'I've been waiting an hour. Not like Kelly.' She got to the door in one quick movement to get the last of the sun. From behind she looked childlike and the matching huge green silk bow pinned to the back of her hair made her oddness vulnerable.

'She'd be Edith Piaf if she hadn't passed on,' said Mia.

The hotel was gleaming, clean and bright with a dining room known for its good food and affordable prices, popular with the locals. Lining the mirrored walls, glass shelves crowded with dozens of bottles in orderly rows, that gave off a clear light, reflected endlessly.

The receptionist checked Cynthia in as part of the group which would begin the following morning, 10 sharp. 'Kelly Brooke usually takes breakfast outside one of the cafes opposite.'

Mia said she would check in for the programme and asked for the tour leader. She would offer the art exchange deal directly with her.

4

'Not possible right now because she hasn't yet arrived.' It was 7 p.m. and Mia asked for a room in the meantime but the receptionist said she'd get a better price if she booked as one of the group.

A well-dressed American woman approached Mia and introduced herself as Lily Bing. 'Ms Brooke is no tour leader but a global celebrity and teacher and a privilege to work with.' She thought the tour was overbooked and there were no rooms left. Cynthia said if it came to it Mia could share her room. Cynthia asked if Lily had been on previous tours.

'All of them. I've read all her books. She's the best.' She paused. 'You've obviously heard of her.' Cynthia might have. 'Deepak Chopra mean anything?' Cynthia made do with a nod of her tired head. 'They are close,' Lily assured her. 'It was Deepak who nicknamed Kelly "The Cat".'

With effort Cynthia was moving her bags towards the lift.

'The Cat is very physical. Gets you working on all dimensions. The known, the unknown. You experience the unseen. You are no longer just vertical or horizontal. She gets us through the portal. She runs at an incredible speed, through the sound barrier. She goes faster and into other dimensions.'

The very thought of it made Cynthia sink down onto a plump lobby couch. 'As long as I don't have to run through the sound barrier.' Her ankles were puffed.

Lily stopped talking as she noticed Mia dragged her luggage to the lift. Surely it wasn't that heavy. 'I hope you ladies are not too...' She paused. '...Mature.'

'Definitely not,' and Mia took the stairs rather than the lift, three flights and running. She paid for that proud jaunt and with knee jolted out of place made it to Cynthia's room on all fours.

Chapter 2

By 8 o'clock when the leader had still not arrived, they decided on an early dinner. Lily was already seated in the hotel dining room. She was well turned out in a high fashion cocktail dress with her hair arranged and coiffed to rest obediently in a bun on top of her head. Cleverly applied makeup almost concealed the ravages of the journey. She'd arrived from LA at 6 that morning after a 20-hour travel strewn with problems and was now fighting off jet lag as she waited for Kelly Brooke. She looked as though she was prepared for an event at the White House rather than dinner with two grand-mothers in a little-known city in North East Spain.

Cynthia came to the table and said she was appalled. 'My mobile doesn't work.' Mia offered hers but it didn't work either.

'There's no signal,' said Lily. 'Only certain servers have coverage. Mobiles from the UK do not usually work because of the mountains.'

Cynthia was beyond appalled. She would have to get a local mobile phone. Was there anywhere still open? Who spoke English around here? The receptionist came to the table smiling and said English was not the problem. The group would be Cynthia's prob-lem. 'No mobiles allowed on Kelly Brooke's tour so you only have to get through this evening. You start early tomorrow.'

Cynthia looked at Mia. 'What about you?'

That was not a problem for Mia, she realized, as most of her close friends were dead. She almost said, 'People die around me like flies.'

'Look, you won't need a mobile,' said Lily.

Cynthia's eyes closed with exasperation.

'If you use a mobile on Kelly Brooke's course, she'll tell you to make the next call to God. So, let's sit down and eat.'

'How about the spa?' said Cynthia.

'Yes, they have intermittent service there but the same guideline applies.'

'I doubt it,' said Cynthia. 'I need this phone.'

'You do seem attached,' said Lily. 'You obviously need this course.'

'Has anyone actually seen Kelly Brooke?' asked Mia. The dining room was almost empty. Only a few tourists were being served, it was too early for the locals.

'She'll be here.' And the American woman opened the menu and pointed out the popular dishes. Mia asked if Kelly had to come far.

Lily did hesitate before saying, 'Miss Brooke will be ready to go 10 o'clock sharp tomorrow morning.'

The hesitation was enough for Mia to go to reception and get one of the last rooms. She asked for it to be on the same arrangement as the rest of the group. The tour leader's lateness was not her problem. Although she rarely spoke Spanish anymore, she was still fluent with the important questions. 'Where is she?' The receptionist didn't know. 'She was supposed to greet Cynthia when she arrived at 5 this afternoon. And where are the others?'

'People come from afar to see her. The group is already booked so don't worry.' She checked the screen. 'At least 15.' She gave her a key to a single room next to Cynthia and said she'd adjust the price.

For one carefree moment Mia was going to ask if she knew of Sal Roca, the love of her youth. He was the first warm person she'd ever met. He was kind, all embracing. With him nothing bad could happen. Light around him gave no place for harm.

She took the key from the receptionist before she gave in to unwise questions and quickly went back to her present life. By the time she reached the table her knee was swollen and she was limping. Cynthia was halfway through a large glass of full-bodied red wine and enjoying every moment. 'I needed that.'

'I hope not,' said Lily. 'No alcohol on these tours. Miss Brooke doesn't allow it.'

'Don't be silly,' said Cynthia and refilled her glass. She examined Mia's knee and said an icepack would get the swelling down. She asked the waiter for ice cubes in a plastic bag.

Over the dinner of Escudella, the regional broth with meat dumpling, followed by seasonal fresh asparagus and 'fideus' — noodles cooked with prawns and served with a garlic sauce — the women introduced themselves and kept it high end. After hearing Cynthia's account of her life in the country which gave her the richness of a close family and also freedom to do what she wanted, not to mention the still youthful successful husband, Mia could no longer afford to be a has-been past her best with two lonely last years to prove it. Her successful times as an artist in London knitted together with those in LA and there were no gaps for any of the despondency and failure to show through. And even sitting here in this unknown hotel with these new strangers was powered by her keenness to create an impression. She was looking for a new style to her work for an exhibition the following year. She elaborated a little more on the story she had already told Cynthia. The exhibition became global.

'So, your work will also be on show in London?' said Cynthia. 'My husband must see it. He snaps up new talent. He's got an eye for it.' She almost added—'Especially in the bedroom.' She decided to put the wine aside in favour of mineral water and prudence.

'In London,' Mia agreed. 'And LA.'

'Oh great!' said Lily. 'Which gallery? I'll be there. I live there.'

On thin ice now Mia named a venue she had got her movie star, art class clients into on occasion. She said something about having to decide in which city to start the show so nothing was quite firmed up. And she quickly turned the conversation around to Lily and what she did in LA.

'I work at Cedar-Sinai.'

Mia knew the hospital only too well as during her marriage to the drug-fuelled rock-star it became his second home. Lily wasn't a nurse. Admin possibly.

'I run a new research department sponsored by a pharmaceutical company.'

Both Cynthia and Mia were impressed and said so.

She also looked after an ageing aunt but didn't mention that.

'So how did you get into this sort of thing? Transformation.' said Cynthia.

'I came across Kelly Brooke on the 'net and read one of her books and did a tour. And this became my life. Makes everything else possible.' Lily got the attention back to Mia. 'So, what kind of art?'

'Oil on canvas.'

'Yes, I must have heard of you,' said Cynthia. She hadn't. But she had heard of the rock-star husband who'd died on drugs. 'He was incredible.'

'Amazing,' said Lily. 'The voice. He had such a range. A bit before my time but as a teenager I loved his songs.' It was now time to say she wasn't married and looked after her aunt. She said she was 54.

'Oh, you're a child,' said Cynthia.

Although Lily said she wouldn't have her life any other way it sounded lonely. Cynthia's life came out the best. The wine helped.

'So, you are well married but free,' Mia told her. 'How come?'

'Because he's in the city all week and I'm in the country. Weekends are family time unless he's on a business trip.'

'Don't you mind him going away so much?'

On that occasion Cynthia described it as a gift. 'The gift of freedom. I can do what I like and wouldn't have it otherwise.' She hoped the unexpected tell-tale tear followed by several more would be interpreted as a slight allergy to the prawns.

And then Cynthia confused the women completely by taking the opposite tack and saying she couldn't be out of reach of a phone because he could call her at any time needing to know where she was and what she was doing. Even her hair flattened with the audacity of the lies.

How free is that? thought Mia.

'So, I have to go upstairs now because he will call for sure to check I have arrived.'

'They'll bring the phone to the table,' said Lily. 'So have a dessert. It's nice having been able to share our lives. We couldn't do it if Kelly Brooke was here.'

Mia asked why not.

'The group starts in the present and stays there. One hour at a time. Transformation has no place for gossip or storytelling, ego or rivalry. We start new and end newer. We embrace the moment.'

'No casual conversation or chat in the dorm. And no drink. Tough,' said Cynthia.

Mia liked the idea. She felt she could go sinking safe into moments and more moments, ending in a single timeless consciousness. 'It's

9

like being sucked down into a warm known space without thought,' she said.

Lily looked at her with interest. 'You will certainly get to a place outside of your daily consciousness.'

'Maybe the time before birth,' said Mia.

'Sounds like a very effective tranquilliser,' said Cynthia. Then she fell in love with the local dessert and ordered another. Crème Caramel with toasted top. Her eyes were closing with exhaustion and a certain sugary delight. How sad her joy of the evening could not be repeated. Lily agreed Kelly Brooke was firm on eating habits.

'Diet you mean?' said Cynthia. 'A horrible word.'

'She wants us to be at our right weight, right shape. It's not called a diet but a preference.'

The local digestif, Ratafia, was not a drink Mia remembered from 25 years ago. It had a pleasant taste, deceptively light. The waiter described it as a mixture of caramel, liquorice, herbs, cinnamon, nutmeg, lemons, mint and rosemary, suitable for most illnesses and good for children. It was a tonic. Lily, with good natural sight, read the label and said it was at least 30% proof. Might do the illnesses in but what happened to the children?

They took their coffees outside to a table on the still busy pedestrian pathway and Cynthia asked what kind of people came to the group. There was no kind. The clients wanted to experience more than the four dimensions they were still in. Time made it four.

'Yes,' said Mia thoughtfully. 'I always thought we are padlocked at birth. Break the lock and be free.' The Ratafia was doing its stuff.

'Are they smart?' said Cynthia. 'I mean do they dress up and go out in the evening?'

'Most of us are sporty and casual. Boots for the mountains. Dress for dinner? A matter of choice. Time to get things ready.' She stood up and although exhausted was fiercely loyal to The Cat and the group and would stay in the foyer to greet any arrivals however late. 'We always start with Happy Hour and that's the one time you get alcohol. I have to lay out the glasses and put the champagne on ice.'

'Oh, please don't do all that if it's just us,' said Cynthia. She mentioned again the calls from her husband and how she'd take them upstairs. Mia realized she didn't have that problem. No one would be calling to see if she had arrived. Cynthia actually dreaded the room and being alone. And having to face a large group of dieting non-drinking strangers, well read in the 'mystery schools' and divinations. All she really wanted was a good laugh.

She didn't know then that she was going to get it.

Mia insisted on trying to identify the group and asked if the people were professional.

'A teacher now and then. Some in the alternative field. Travellers. Others on their way to Santiago de Compostela. Occasional Corporate wanting a break. Others wanting to change their lives.' Lily left to lay out the glasses.

Mia found standing up difficult and her knee hot and inflamed. It was the Blue Hour, the lights luminous and clear. People passing along the pedestrian pathway looked good in themselves and some greeted or smiled at Cynthia. She did have a certain allure and looked as though she could be someone well known.

'I am not altogether looking forward to Kelly The Cat,' she said. 'Apart from the ban on alcohol, gossip, egos and rivalry, there's that careful diet and all this going into other realities. I have enough trouble with this one. And spiritual knowhow. I don't know about you but I don't have the vocabulary let alone composure for any of it.'

Mia had been in Hollywood too long to be concerned. 'It will all come down to breathing. It always does. Whatever you pay.'

Cynthia was doubtful. 'I think you need to know the language for this sort of thing. Yin Yang doesn't quite do it. Is she Buddhist? And what strain, or whatever it's called, does she practice?'

'We can ask her. When and if she finally gets here.'

'Lily is optimistic. She's put out 20 glasses at least and redone her makeup.' Cynthia sank back in her chair and looked at the full moon. 'It's got an aura. I haven't really looked at the moon for a while. My eyes pass over things but I don't really see them. "What is this world if, full of care/We have no time to stand and stare." ' She kicked off her shoes and rested her feet on a chair. She did seem to let go and absorb the evening. And they sat breathing in the sweet scent carried by the southerly wind. Suddenly Cynthia had to go upstairs as she was certain the phone calls from her husband had not been put through. By now he would be concerned and she shivered as though her body was actually attached to his concern.

Concerned? Or curious? Mia wondered. But Cynthia looked as though forbidden trysts were long past.

'These types like my husband take a lot of work.' Cynthia jigged her fingers through her mass of sun-bleached hair making it more exuberant. 'I've spoilt him. He won't sleep if he doesn't know....' — she looked at her thin gold watch —'...what I'm doing,' she continued lifelessly.

Mia reminded her it was an hour earlier in the UK.

'9 p.m. He will be watching CNN then reach for the brandy I had the sense to hide. He's got to keep his blood pressure down. And the shirts from the laundry are still in my room.' She got up and gathered her jacket, bag, shoes, and room key. 'It really is beautiful out here. I just want to see the moon as it comes through the trees. It is a special place. I can see why they bring seekers here.' And as if to charm her more all the bells rang out the hour.

She still didn't want to leave the table in the now obvious moonlight. Mia was going to suggest she keep it simple and just phone him.

It was as though she'd brought her husband, at least his presence, to the table and Mia was audience to Cynthia's concern for a way of life with a man she implied she was lucky to have captured. He was someone of importance and not afraid of his power, drop-dead gorgeous but somehow elusive. What would Miss Brooke think of all this making an absent man the centre of the 'now'? Mia came to realize he was present only through Cynthia's delivery. This man was hers or even a part of her and you would find out only what she chose to show you. He could want his brandy or his TV programmes recorded or being driven by his wife fast to an airport in their ultimate car. You would get this in simple statements but no more. Mia did wonder after a while if he really existed. Now that Cynthia turned, hair lifting, curls coiling, to get to the room, where the phone was sure to ring, Mia realized one thing — Mr and Mrs Coy had separate rooms — only his laundry in hers.

Upstairs in her hotel room Cynthia unpacked and wondered why she had to behave as she had. Her husband would only ring if there was a national emergency. He would be out enjoying his freedom and her absence. She thought she must keep a good face on it all. Don't tell this unknown artist anything. 'Thank God she didn't suggest I phone him. The only good thing about it.' And for no reason she sat on the bed and started shaking with tears. And down in the narrow, cobbled streets Mia thought, I like her although she's not my sort. These tough English women! Bet she's never had a rough day.

Chapter 3

Cynthia came back down to the foyer because she had some cold compresses and homeopathic cream for Mia's knee. The truth was she could not bear to be alone in that room. Of course, she'd tried to phone her husband but he was not at home and his mobile was switched off. 'How do you feel about the stand-in for Ms Brooke?' said Cynthia.

Mia thought Lily would calm down once the woman actually arrived.

'I didn't like her attitude about the mobile phone. I won't be doing this tour if this goes on,' continued Cynthia.

'Oh, you must!' Mia sounded over-enthusiastic but a few painting sessions might actually hold the imminent money problem at bay.

Cynthia put the cream onto Mia's knee and covered it with a compress. 'Should do the trick. I use it on my husband.'

Mia felt if she heard 'my husband' one more time she'd resort to the Ratafia bottle. If he was going to be part of their exchanges and Mia thought he was, she'd better know his name.

'Ed Coy.'

She liked the name and asked what he did.

'Investment.' That covered a lot of ground.

Cynthia had had a shower, washed her hair, changed her clothes and felt marginally better. But she could not be alone. 'Are all those for us?' She pointed at the glasses and champagne buckets when Lily came back.

Lily said members of the group were due in from Barcelona and others were coming by car. Mia asked if there was any sign of Kelly Brooke. Lily opened another bottle as though she hadn't heard.

Mia asked the girl at reception if she had actually spoken to Miss Brooke. She said she had.

'We seem to be only three in this group.'

14

'There's at least two upstairs sleeping.'

And then Mia did wonder if this was part of the deal—new character-challenging courses that had replaced for many the boring holidays in exhausted resorts. They did include testing practices. How do you manage a few let-down moments on arrival? How do you deal with the unfamiliar? Hate on sight? Or a big favourite—the wrong room. These alternative breaks had begun even when Mia was in Hollywood.

Lily decided to take the women's minds off Ms Brooke and onto themselves.

'Is your diet sugar-free?'

'Of course not,' said Cynthia.

Lily topped up Cynthia's glass and spent some moments on the downfall of the good old comforter, sugar. She said the group dropped the intake daily. 'Do you know cancer cannot survive in a sugar-free body?'

Cynthia was not having it. Mia said she'd think about it. A few more questions and Lily had filled in the enrolment sheet. 'Any health problems?'

'None on this occasion,' said Cynthia.

Lily asked if she practised any kind of meditation.

She didn't.

Lily asked what she did do.

'I do horses.'

Lily stood up and saw the pedestrian passageway still lively. 'Let's go and have a walk in the old part and...'

'I couldn't,' said Cynthia.

Lily was alert. 'So how much exercise do you take daily?'

'None,' said Cynthia.

Mia had done her share in Hollywood but the displaced knee from the show-off run up the stairs earlier was a measure of what she once did but did no longer.

Lily rearranged the glasses. 'I'm waiting for two people coming by car and another from Barcelona airport.'

And then Mia thought she had the answer. Kelly Brooke probably

15

had an A-list guest and had gone to the airport in Barcelona to meet him or her. And the plane was delayed. Mia had done enough of that with the movie-star painters in LA. Lily said an actor was coming from a movie break in Canada.

'Who?' said Cynthia promptly.

'Kelly likes to make the introductions. But he'll go anywhere to work with her.' She looked at Mia's knee. 'I want you to take it easy. You're not spring chickens. Either of you.' She stood up ready for the walk and decided to finish off the bottle. 'I haven't had such a good evening for ages. And so much to drink! While I look like this, I hope The Cat won't show up.'

No chance of that.

Two women struggled through the revolving door with substantial luggage. They'd arrived at Barcelona airport from Kentucky and as there was no transport at this hour took a taxi the last 60kms of the journey at great expense. Lily was deeply relieved. Perennial group members, they were the real thing. They were given champagne before their rucksacks left their shoulders.

'Now Happy Hour starts ticking,' said Lily. There followed some moments of friendly exchange. These women were seasoned travellers and had been on the road three months through South America by various means of transport. They talked with awe of the mountains in Peru, the jungles in Columbia. 'You can't get tougher than that. Or more isolated. Didn't see a person for a week. Saw everything else.' Rachel, a dental nurse from Kansas had always promised that when she reached 40, she'd hit the road and never look back. 'Couldn't have done it without Kelly Brooke and the groups.' Her travelling companion Abigail, who in search of the feeling of freedom had taken a sabbatical from teaching at Rutgers University New York, had joined Rachel on her journey.

'South America beat the road trip we did last year in Australia,' said Rachel. 'That in comparison was surface experience. Next we take the old train across Russia.' She was weathered and sunburned and a little travel worn. Abigail in comparison looked as though she took care of herself. She was still pretty with a light energy, her skin pale, translucent, eyes bright and clear. Travel exhaustion had made no dent in her appearance.

Cynthia asked Abigail what made her want to travel.

'I read Kerouac, *On the Road*. On this trip got into William Burroughs.'

'Oh, you would,' cut in Lily pleased. 'I knew you would travel.' She took hold of Abigail's hand. 'You are going to be reborn. It's all going to be better.'

And Mia got the feeling the travelling teacher had gone through quite a lot before she started on the road reading Burroughs.

Suddenly the new arrivals, worn out, said goodnight.

'Breakfast as usual,' said Rachel. 'Outside on the patio in the sun. One of my best memories.'

Lily hurried after them with two large bottles of mineral water. 'Drink plenty. Don't dehydrate. Keep your feet raised so your ankles don't swell and before you go to sleep a little meditation.'

Esmee, the diminutive French performer, still in the green silk dress, crossed the foyer. She waved a greeting but her eyes saw only the champagne. 'I like champagne,' she said. That was no lie. 'I have come to appreciate Prosecco; people say they prefer it to champagne. They prefer the price maybe. Prosecco is a juvenile wine that used to do the trick when you couldn't afford the real thing. But we must not even compare it to champagne. I admit I have made quite an evening of it. Old friends and too many old bars.'

'Maybe you should go to bed,' said Lily.

'Are you crazy?!' Esmee took over the pouring of the drinks.

'I just realized who she is,' whispered Cynthia. 'Esmee Pont. She was quite a name.'

Mia didn't know her.

'It must be her. A singer in the 1950s. Always on the bill with the French star, Charles Trenet.' Cynthia sang one of the Frenchman's hits.

Esmee turned around smiling. '*Le Mer*, so you remember Charles Trenet?'

'I remember you,' said Cynthia.

Esmee made no comment and turned back to the unfinished

17

champagne. At some point in her boisterous evening the green bow had slid down sideways, almost lost. It had met trouble in some dark alley and one proud silk skein was spotted with ash and street dirt. 'So how many are we this time? Are they all drinking in the Arc Bar?'

Arc Bar resounded down through Mia's memory. The bar she had loved in her youth.

Lily declined another refill. 'Don't be so silly,' said Esmee and poured it anyway. 'Ms Brooke doesn't let us enjoy things too much. Physical things. So, let's make the most of her unusual absence. On these little tours everyone has a night before the long days that follow and all of them dry. Her groups, always overbooked, are sought after. She keeps them small. They are not like the groups the American writers bring. Forty seated along the table with a pre-set menu.'

'Luis ran the Arc Bar,' Mia said suddenly. How could she have forgotten the Arc, even more, let it slip from her existence? She saw the present moment was a mere mean pinch of time focused on survival compared with the multi-layered colourful past. 'It was the first bar of its kind open till dawn, playing the great American jazz and Luis cooked sausages on the grill and wore shades even at night. It was always full. There was no one like him. Eloquent, witty, understood politics, loved gossip.'

Esmee turned. 'If you wanted to know something you went to Luis. It was his city. You must have been here a few years ago to know Luis.'

Mia agreed and almost mentioned Sal Roca but that had to be another conversation, some other time.

Cynthia asked about the other tours.

'The Americans do the same old well-trod route. Thirty in a coach to see the Black Madonna in Monserrat.'

'Monserrat,' Cynthia cut in. 'My husband liked that idea.'

What was it about 'my husband' that Mia couldn't bear? Perhaps the fact she didn't have one. 'Let's just call him Ed.'

'It's a sharp drive up?' Cynthia asked. 'He's not keen on tight curves.' She stopped. Of course, that's just what he was keen on. She had voiced his preference casually, quite lackadaisical. Maybe it was time for her to go to a shrink and voice the lot. Pull out all his preferences. He had slept with 2000 women but no longer with her. It was, it seemed about to come out, inconsequentially in the language of every day.

She fled into the memory of her kitchen, perhaps the one place of safety in her entire life. Her fierce concentration brought this green belt existence straight into the foyer of the Catalan hotel which became filled with 'the aga', 'the old mangle belonging to my mother', and well-to-do friends dropping in with names like 'Rufus' and 'Dottie'. And the traditional Catalan mirrors and clocks, the lamps and paintings with no strength to fight for attention were losing their hold on reality, were disappearing from sight. Even the green silk bow, half hanging in the performer's hair, had lost its place. Mia could virtually see Cynthia's old Mrs Beaton cookery books and the cleaning woman with the old-fashioned rough cloth 'doing the floors'. 'She likes the old down-to-earth ways,' explained Cynthia. 'Those sponges on sticks as she calls them, don't do a proper job.' Mia could smell the roast in the oven, the sage and garlic.

'So, what is the focus of the group?' Lily asked and looked at Mia. 'What do you think?' Mia had no idea.

'Seeking the metaphysical mysteries,' Esmee told her. 'Having been here in those special days you would know of those.'

Cynthia had another idea. 'The ones who come here have probably been just across the border to Rennes-le-Château to find out how a poor priest in 1892, between a day and a night, became a millionaire.'

Esmee took the story over from her — after all she was French. 'The mystery became global and gave rise to bestsellers, TV, movies. And they can't get any further. The story's worn out. They can't solve the mystery. So, seekers come here to Girona where the mysteries remain unsolved but fresh. They want to experience practices, prophecies, rituals, so secrets become part of the group activity.'

'Or they want to express something individually,' said Mia. How she hoped they did, so she could start the painting group. 'Through writing or better, painting, they make actual what they discern.'

'I was thinking about that,' said Cynthia. 'I personally would love to paint.' Loyal to Mia she added that they had a painter right there at their table.

Esmee stayed with the Rennes-le-Château idea. 'People have read the books, seen the movies, made the visit to the priest's house, the tower, the church. They go away empty. They don't know how to look. That is what Kelly Brooke can show us. How to look.'

'How much is the group?' Mia wished she hadn't asked. Lily gave a figure which would give a sleepless night.

'It sounds a lot,' said Lily, 'But it is ten days. Kelly works fast and gets you on the etheric plane. You become who you should be. You'll say it's worth double. Ask the ones who are coming. Ask Esmee.'

She signed the dinner bill. 'My treat,' she told Mia. 'It's great you and Cynthia are here. We don't usually have two ... mature women .' She nearly said 'old'.

Cynthia nudged Mia and looking at the French woman whispered, 'If we're mature what is she?'

'Hiding 80.'

They took their drinks outside and a sudden breeze made the atmosphere joyful. 'A wind from the south,' Mia said. 'Always lucky for me.' She realized it was what Sal Roca always told her.

Three group members had arrived by car, checked in and gone straight to bed. Cynthia tried to keep track of Lily's information but kept falling asleep.

'So, the groups are seeking the metaphysical,' said Mia. 'This place certainly lends itself to that. It has mysteries on every corner.'

Lily gave Mia a meditation practice to try before sleep, and Cynthia woke up. 'As long as I haven't been snoring.'

Lily woke her enough to make the journey to the lift and together with Mia got her to bed.

'As long as I don't snore. He dreads that.'

'I wonder if he rang,' said Mia suddenly. 'The husband.'

'He won't with Kelly around,' said Lily. 'First part of the course is detachment and boundaries. You'll love it.'

'If I can pay for it,' and Mia went back downstairs.

Chapter 4

The foyer was full of chattering new arrivals from the States. They knew each other from previous visits, and tiredness and jet lag had no place in their enthusiasm. A few went outside to hear the bells of the city chime midnight. It was a real welcome.

'I really want to go back to the Dolmen this time.' The woman's voice was strident New York and she was used to getting her way. She was possibly middle-aged, smart, dressed impeccably, well-coiffed and beautifully made up. She was money and time packaged distinctly. 'Oh yes,' said the young guy taking shots with a substantial camera. 'Let's ask Kelly to put that on first. It's not such good weather later in the week.' The receptionist told Mia he was Eric Haas, a well-known documentary maker from NY.

'But where is she?' said the elegant woman. 'Where is Kelly? Surely she'd be here to greet us.'

The side door crashed open and serious luggage skidded into the foyer.

'My God,' said Eric Haas. 'They've come for the duration. They really are going to settle here.'

Two women from Baltimore, tough and looking for a night of fun, followed the line of boxes and crates and chucked the last bags into corners. With a whoop of joy, they hugged Eric and then Lily, Esmee, everybody known and otherwise.

'Have you come for good?' asked the receptionist.

'For bad,' said Josie, the smaller one wearing a cap and braces. 'Let's make a night of it.' They hugged the staff coming out to meet them.

'Now the party really starts,' announced Lily and champagne corks popped appropriately.

Eric put the women's luggage onto a trolley. 'All these bags! All these objects! Who carries this huge menopausal luggage? It's a life decider. You'll have to live here.'

The couple from Baltimore were overweight, rowdy, sleepless. 'Sleep is the cousin of death,' said the bigger one, Lew with cropped hair, wearing a man's vest, her skin crowded with tattoos. 'So, bring on the star. Where's she hiding? Come out, Kelly. Frightened you've aged? We've all aged. Don't worry. We've been 20 hours on the road to see you.'

Lily with heightened colour and too bright eyes courtesy of tiredness and drink said, 'Now The Cat will come.' She turned to the new arrivals. 'Josie and Lew are here.' She went to the desk and started making phone calls. 'It's good news. She'll be here in seven minutes.'

'The plane landed late,' said Josie and rubbed her partner's tattooed arms. 'We took a cab from Barcelona airport so we'd catch her.'

'From the airport to here?' Eric was impressed. 'How much was that?'

'The price would scare you,' said Lew. 'And we paid double 'cos we asked him to make it fast and he did it in an hour. I've brought The Cat some presents.' She dug in a bag and pulled out a large pink cardboard box. 'I got it when I was in India last month. Full of the perfume she likes.' She tugged at a bunch of framed photos. 'And all these. Cat with Bowie. Cat with Deepak. Cat with just herself and the mirror.'

Mia sat on the last available chair slightly outside the group and weighed up her chances of being able to give them a painting class. The score – Cynthia 1, the foyer friends 0. It couldn't get worse. It could. She recognized the tattooed woman. She and her partner were well-known artists and made big money. Friends of Hockney. Mia recalled their painting and how she disliked it.

'Where is The Cat?' Lew was impatient. 'We've been here at least a minute.'

Lily filled their hands with glasses of champagne and small black cigarettes and Esmee started singing what had evolved over the years as the 'party song'. They all joined in a conga line and danced around the foyer and through the restaurant, and hotel guests, kitchen staff, night walkers from the street joined the swaying line winding its way back through the foyer. It was loud. It was exuberant. It took away all anxiety. Here was a good time and the conga line opened up for Mia and she had danced enough in her time to take it beyond the constrictions of a damaged knee. And sing she could with all her heart and the pulsing, tireless line went out through the open street door and along the shadowed alleys to the iron bridge. Had Kelly Brooke joined in? Surely this was her optimum arrival moment.

Back in a broken line they hip-hopped, boogied or jived the last few moments, then sunk sweating and laughing onto the sofas, the floor. Esmee gave them all a song of welcome. Then they asked for other French favourites and she chose a Piaf classic. Sometime after that in a calm interlude a night porter put on his favourite jazz, Coltrane, and started preparing the group's favourite tissanes and coffee with brandy — it was going to be a long night. The Cat was still not there. Lily again went to reception and used the phone. The news was still good. 'Here in four minutes.'

'Where is she exactly?' The elegant woman directed the question at Eric.

'I don't know, Maggie. I'm not clairvoyant tonight.'

'The leader is usually greeting us at the door ready with the itinerary and collecting the cash.' Some of the others made signs of agreement.

Eric saved it. 'Kelly is fabulous. And she has only fabulous moments. Right now, she's engaged in a truly awesome meditation that she's trying out for us. It's going to lift us to other heights we have not reached before. She's completing this, tying the knot, for us. How can we equate time with Kelly Brooke? How can we imprison her in a clock? Tick-tock. She deals with stuff out there beyond time.'

Nice try, Eric, thought Mia.

'Well yes, Eric,' said Maggie, her voice rasping. 'But what do we do, us lot, prisoners of time? If we go on sitting here waiting, we'll be grandmothers next.'

The two from Baltimore were on their feet. 'Magic hour. Let's hit a few night spots. The Arc Bar will still be open and the Sunset Club never shuts.'

'Or that club by the old church of St Pilar,' said Eric getting up.

There was a general exodus to the street and they trod the ancient stones of the old quarter carelessly in search of cheap joy.

Mia sat stunned. This was her town. She was there from the first moments of the Arc Bar opening. Luis, Sal Roca and the others pushed open the seventeenth century door and told her, 'Welcome traveller, this is your destination.' Emilio was there and Gloria. She would have to fill in the rest of the names. Too many forgotten. It was a very particular remarkable time. And now these interlopers were claiming these places as theirs. She was so sad she considered going up and waking Cynthia.

And then Eric was beside her, his hand over hers. He said sweetly, 'It's your first time with this group. It gets better.' He laughed. 'You'll get used to it. In the end you'll like it.' He lifted her hand and enclosed it in his.

Maggie stood up, her spiky cruel shoes like mathematical equations. 'Eric I'm going to bed. I really do want to visit the Dolmens this time. I knew before I felt some presence or energy there. I have to check it's real because in a funny way it changed my life. So, let's cut all this foyer talk and go together.' Then she saw his hand in Mia's and didn't like it. She got a little closer for a better look. 'I saw your daughter upstairs. I think she thought you'd got lost.'

'As long as I know where I am,' said Mia tartly, 'I'm ahead of the game.'

The foyer had gone quiet.

'Oh my! Surely you are with her ... the one with the lovely blonde hair ... a little chubby?'

Mia looked into the hard, green eyes that held the terrible pain of getting old and the harsh lines no plastic surgery could safely fix. She'd seen it all before in Hollywood. She stood up. Eric eased her back down. 'Leave it. She's a little passed her bedtime.' And to the woman he said, 'Maggie, go up and I'll bring you some hot tea.' To Mia he said, 'That's Margaret de Romillie.' He paused for Mia to know her. She didn't. 'She was Hollywood back in Clifford Odet's time.' He listed her husbands. 'She was a terrific hostess. The *Washington Post* connection didn't do any harm.' Mia had heard the names but didn't know the woman. Eric took her other hand and held them both between his. 'Do you know the Dolmen at Romanyà?'

'Yes, I did. Once.'

'I thought you did.' His smile was true and innocent.

'Why?' she said.

'The way you reacted just now to its name.'

The elegant woman still waited for Eric whose hands were still intertwined with Mia's. The promise of his bringing hot tea to her room didn't quite do it. The clocks in the foyer ticked towards danger. Mia didn't want a problem, especially one that wasn't hers. She slid away from him, stood up and crossed to the lift. 'Is she really on her way this time?' she said as she passed Lily. The woman didn't even pause. 'She's already at the end of the street.' Mia still pressed the lift button.

'She's worth waiting for.'

Mia was too wired to go to bed. Passing Cynthia's door, she listened for snoring. She heard speaking. 1 a.m. Was she talking in her sleep? Then she decided Cynthia might finally want to meet The Cat and knocked on the door. Cynthia was awake and dressed.

'The Legend expected in four minutes.'

'The party was so loud I couldn't sleep. It sounded great so I got ready to come down. Then I got a call.'

'Your husband?'

She did pause. 'My daughter. It sounds so good down there I'll come with you. It's like the old days. The parties. I never bothered going to bed.'

'Nor did I,' said Mia.

Chapter 5

They got the best chairs and a small table before the others came back from the clubs. Cynthia talked about her life, lucky and full but she needed a break. 'I'm getting older.' Mia asked how old. '57.' She'd been saying that for years. Even the number seemed worn out. Mia talked about Hollywood, her art, her modelling, her teaching and Cynthia was cheered up. 'You've really done something with your life.' She was so enthusiastic she decided to celebrate with a little rosé wine. 'I wouldn't mind something to keep going. One of those breads smeared with oil and ham.' Mia agreed. The night porter thought the kitchen was closed. Eric was swiftly beside them and said Lily would arrange it. 'It's only 1 o'clock. Do you want a little omelette to go with it?'

'Might as well,' said Cynthia. 'By the way, where is Lily? I've stopped asking about the other one.'

'And let's have some olives,' said Mia.

Esmee joined them and said Cynthia had lovely hair and stroked it back off her face. 'You're a good-looking woman. Robust. You know what you want.'

'Will I get it? That's the question these days.' She turned to Mia. 'May as well have a little of the red wine too.'

Everything about the order was 'little' and as though to take away any thought that these two women of a certain age were greedy overeaters, and possibly lushes as well.

'It's an unusual night. It could be any time,' said Cynthia. Even the reception clock had stopped. Eric sat beside them and outlined the itinerary from the start of the course at 10 o'clock sharp in the cafe opposite. 'Introduction, walking meditation, yin yoga, lunch. She gives her talks after lunch, then come the practises. Tomorrow psychometry. She's keen on that. After a walk in the country or more correctly a power walk...'

Cynthia interrupted and said she didn't like that.

26

Eric put a bottle of mineral water on the table and got some glasses. 'We drink a lot of mineral water. We detox as we go.'

Lily laid the table and the night porter brought the food. 'Do you want Django Reinhardt?'

Cynthia blinked. 'The musician. Is he here too?'

'I'll put on a few tracks from my collection while you eat,' said the night porter.

They all agreed they liked Django Reinhardt.

'Deep relaxation, then enquiry, dinner early, for Spain,' Eric continued. 'Because the workshops start at 10 and finish midnight on the dot, she likes an early start.'

'Early?' said Cynthia.

'7 a.m.'

'Never!' Cynthia knew her limitations.

'You could tone up and lose a little weight,' Eric said taking a chance.

'I could. But my husband likes me this way. What kind of people come to these groups?'

Eric described a diverse selection. 'They all have one thing in common. Adventure.'

'And well-off,' said Cynthia. 'The price would make anyone think twice.'

Eric did not disagree. 'It sets the tone. Guarantees a certain integrity.'

Cynthia tried to catch Mia's attention but something about his last remark lifted her up off the chair and over to reception. The girl from earlier in the night was back on duty. 'I need to reach Ms Brooke.' It was something about the integrity. If she could use that she might be saved. 'It's something I need to offer her but she has to make up her mind now.' The girl said it was impossible.

'Eight hours late! Don't you think you should check-up? Maybe there's been an accident.' The girl said the night porter would deal with it and she should eat her food. 'We will take care of everything. Don't worry.'

Mia wasn't worried about the delayed Ms Brooke. She was worried about everything else.

It was about 2 a.m. when they noticed a small man with an egg-shaped head walking up and down the foyer. He seemed out of place. He'd be out of place anywhere, Mia decided. His face had no visible bone structure. Two eyes, a nose, a slit of mouth. It amounted to a children's drawing of a grownup. Humpty Dumpty, he moved as though life was a joke. He wore a suit, smart shoes and one bright mauve sock, ill-fitting, which had slipped down the side of his left shoe. The other was neatly out of sight. His hand-knitted sweater was also of a mauve colour that brought out the worst in the suit. A smattering of thin black hair rested on his head. It looked temporary. Tomorrow it would fade to grey, fall out and be gone. He couldn't be metaphysical. No, he could not be one of the group. Mia decided he was some sort of a salesman. 'He's been kept awake by all the noise,' said Cynthia. Then she described her life in the English countryside and how she organized the local WI.

Lily, confused said, 'WI? Is that military?'

'Women's groups. We work through issues.'

'Kelly Brooke works through everything,' promised Lily. 'You will find out claustrophobia is something you get over. Vertigo, an app on your software you don't need.'

It was then they noticed the walking man had paused and was listening. 'But where is she?' Cynthia was now exhausted.

'Probably doing some special preparation. She can meditate and travel far.'

'I wish she'd just travel here,' said Cynthia in a tone her husband disliked. 'What about the spa?'

'Day after tomorrow. You've never seen anything like it. It's old, before Roman times. Wonderful atmosphere.' Lily turned to the walking man. 'Are you keeping awake for an early flight? I've done that a few times.'

'No. Just waiting.' He was English, hard to place, with a small smart voice with rough edges, an ill-concealed legacy from less smart origins. He asked if it was possible to get something to eat. Close up he looked as though quite a lot had happened to him over the years. His face was grey with fatigue, his smile a surprise, kind, making everything else momentarily radiant. Lily arranged for reception to

28

order a ham sandwich with a side of tomato and olives. He introduced himself—'Dick Topper,' and said he had booked weeks ago.

'Booked what?' said Lily

'To do the tour.'

Even Lily looked surprised. He just didn't fit. She hid her reaction
as she examined the long list of arrivals. Dick Topper had paid the
required deposit of half fee upfront.

The group was back. The music at the clubs had been great, and they
wanted more. The night porter tried to please them which upset the
guests upstairs trying to sleep. No compromise worked and his
phone rang continually with complaints. In the end Eric said it was
time to sit in meditation followed by an intro talk with great jazz, soft
in the background. He arranged them on chairs, on sofas, on the floor
and his voice leading the meditation was such that the energy level
went calm and easy. Afterwards Cynthia told him he had a wonderful technique. He said he was no Kelly Brooke. 'Chance would be
a fine thing.'

'But where is she?' Lew from Baltimore broke out first.

'She's awesome,' said Josie. 'I totally trust her. There's no one like
her. I mean, Sean is flying over from the States tomorrow on his
private plane with his bodyguards and all the crap as usual, so where
is she?'

'Deep meditation to kick-ass us into shape,' said Lew. 'She'll be
deep into something.'

'Let's do a few intros now,' said Eric. 'Then up to our rooms so
we're ready and rested for our great 10 a.m. start.'

'Hardly,' said Cynthia. 'It's after 2 now. It's not worth going to
bed.'

'Exactly,' said Esmee. 'Nobody goes to bed. We usually greet the
dawn.' She lowered her voice. 'Sean is A-list. Movies. She'll have to
be present for him.'

Eric stood up and gave an introduction about the city of Girona.
During his talk a cluster of arrivals gathered at reception and Lily
indicated she needed help. He carried on talking. 'Something happened here. It happened in Girona because that's the designated

compass reading for such things to happen. It couldn't occur any-where else. It was a moment in this very place where we are gathered. It was a change on the predicted dimensions of this planet. Four dimensions became five and into the gap a frequency occurred that received an object from elsewhere. What was it? A presence? A substance? What components made up this unexpected thing? It became lodged into our planetary system. Its origins and story had been kept here since ages past, since the beginning of known time. Kept, not in the Vatican or Solomon's Temple or the UN but here in this ancient town. At first its story was carved in rock. Then prophecies were received by the soothsayers and later the tribal elders. Its history was etched on papyrus. Inked onto scrolls. It's been in the care not of the church but a private society for hundreds of years. Was the lodging of this object in Catalonia predetermined? Down to fate? Was it meant? A mistake? An accident? This would be the right place because the ley lines are powerful, the frequencies magnetic. This significant place has a vast history going back thousands of years. Beings before the Neanderthal have left an imprint that is recoverable. Of course, the signs are still here of what happened. They are not for everybody. Why? Because people could not receive this knowledge. So, it's been kept over the centuries by a society. There will always be keepers of the secrets. They are here today. Why are we here? To prepare our-selves to receive the secret. This object. Why? Because it takes us into a superior enlightenment. A state of being beyond the locked time of birth and death. That is why we are chosen.'

Cynthia had forced herself to stay awake. By pure willpower, refusing to blink, her eyes watery, mascara running, eyeliner smeared, she had for once heard something she liked. Lily had been signalling to Eric to close down his speech, to bring the subject to a definite close and join her by reception. People milled around the bar, perplexed. Some were thrilled, others impressed.

'It's certainly a good sales gimmick,' said Cynthia. 'And accounts for the high price we're paying.'

Mia realized she had believed it. Knowing the territory as she did, such an occurrence was not impossible. 'It's probably a piece of a star,' she said. 'Or a ... being from out there.'

Others joined in with their impressions. A newly arrived English woman said, 'I thought a comet.' Esmee doubted that. 'Information,' she thought. 'To transform us so we can reach them.'

'Them?' said Cynthia.

'Out there. Why would they want us as we are? We don't even want each other,' said Esmee.

Mia thought that was possibly true.

'This is too much for me,' said Cynthia. 'I'm just here for a rest, some sun and good food. My husband said what I need is a good lover.' She quickly drank some sobering water.

The groups at the bar shifted, making a space and into this SHE appeared, the beautiful one, the cinder black-haired woman, charismatic and almost beyond human. It was just like the story Eric had told. The gap and into it lodged the thing of value. She was too beautiful. Mia nudged Cynthia. 'She's here.' And then she was gone. And Cynthia thought she caught the last of her profile. 'It was her, wasn't it?'

'Must be.' Cynthia hadn't really seen her, just a glimpse. 'But why didn't this lot react? We are talking about The Cat. You think they'd be all over her. At least I'm sure about the French woman. She must be Esmee Pont. She went out with Johnny Halliday. Remember him?'

'Just about. Esmee Pont was around in the '50s and '60s.'

Lily slid into the seat beside them and stopped any questions about The Cat's arrival or anybody's arrival except the gang by the door newly checking in from an exhausting drive. 'We're short of rooms. Seven more people have shown up pre-booked. And you,' she turned to Mia, 'have got one of their rooms, a double, and we need it back till everything's sorted tomorrow.'

'It is tomorrow,' said Cynthia. 'You are welcome to share with me,' she told Mia.' I will get you a key cut before there's any more preferential treatment for friends just turning up.'

'Could you?' said Lily but before anyone could decide Eric joined them.

'There's a woman, one of ours, upstairs who's taken a double when she's alone.'

31

'Eva,' said Lily. 'She's got the other bed for the skull. She's just back from Croatia.'

'Croatia,' echoed Cynthia.

'Visiting the pyramid.' Lily realized Cynthia had no idea about the place or the object.

'A pyramid has been discovered in Croatia more significant than the one in Egypt. Can you girls share or not?' Lily was tricky and strained. She was not the same management girl of nine hours ago who could do well in a crisis. Her skin was pulled tight like a burglar's stocking, eyes looked away, any 'away', as long as her gaze did not contain Cynthia or the English painter.

'Why has she brought back a skull? That's what I was asking.'

'Crystal. It's one of the crystal skulls,' said Esmee. 'There are very few. They are an exact replica of the brain.'

'Why does the skull need a separate bed?' said Cynthia.

'Because it knows everything,' said Lily

'Basically, the skull is psychic,' explained Eric patiently. 'Where Eva goes the skull goes with her.'

'Perhaps if it knows everything,' said Cynthia. 'It would know where Ms Brooke is.'

Lily, beyond patience, shouted, 'Will you two share and let these pre-booked ones get to bed?'

'You lost me,' said Cynthia. 'The skull needs a separate bed and can't just' — she was keeping back laughter at all costs — 'lie on a cushion?'

'Seems so,' said Eric closing his eyes, the laughter building in him uncontrollable.

'Act out of respect,' said Lily snapping now, turning on Eric.

He wiped his eyes and didn't dare look at Cynthia.

'And get those two drinkers in the same room and show some respect at least to Kelly.'

'Don't put it on him,' said Cynthia starting to enjoy herself now.

Eric jumped up, all laughter gone. 'No, no. Lily's right. It's been a long day.'

'Suck up,' hissed Cynthia.

'I moved the new arrivals into Mia's room so get a truckle bed in there.'

'I think Mia needs her own space,' said Eric calmly. How right he was. She could have hugged him.

Lily, definitely edgy now, told him Mia was not even part of the group yet and hadn't paid and would have to relinquish room 155.

'Nice number,' said Esmee at the next table. 'It adds up to 11. I bet some of these in the foyer could do something with number 11. Sacred number.'

'Just sort it out, Eric.' It sounded like a warning. Trying to smile Lily held her hand out for Mia's key.

'Why don't we ask the skull where it wants to sleep,' said Cynthia.

'I think I'll go to my room before I don't have it.' Mia's knee burned and needed attention.

And then there she was, the beautiful one quietly just there in the doorway. It was not clear when she came in. She was simply present, part of the crowd, superbly sure, with an inner elegance. There was no one like her. She looked as though she was staying one night by default and her destination was the multi-star palace with The Rich on Top of The Hill. Mia nudged Cynthia who said, 'Yes I see what they mean by awesome.'

'It is her.'

'Must be,' Cynthia was almost sure.

'I need to do a deal with her.' The woman had moved out of sight. Eric got up. 'I'll have a word with Eva.'

'Why don't you ask Kelly Brooke,' said Cynthia. 'She was here just a few minutes ago.' Lily and Eric looked sincerely surprised. It took their minds off the little matter of overbooked rooms.

'You spoke to her? To Kelly?' Lily sounded cautious.

'There's been a problem with her not being here all evening and half the night and now her being here is a problem,' said Cynthia.

Eric looked at Lily. They had to doubt this development. Eric smiled. 'We're all tired and think we see who we don't.' Cynthia got to her feet and looked around the foyer. The woman was not to be seen. Lily and Eric crossed to reception talking vociferously. Mia tried out the deal on Cynthia. 'I've brought my painting materials and if worst comes to worst case, I can give lessons in payment for the course.' She pointed to the doorway. 'She's there.'

'Oh,' said Cynthia. 'It's like that.' She looked at the doorway to decide if the woman was the open receptive sort. 'Is she a phantom only we see? Nobody's even talking to her.'

When Mia got across to the entrance the woman had gone.

3 a.m. turned to 4 a.m. and there was no more mention of Kelly Brooke and even Lily gave up looking positive. The champagne, a shallow has-been, all out of bubbles, lay acid and lifeless at the bottom of the glasses as though hung over and at the mercy of its own pleasure venom. The ice in the buckets gave in and melted. Eric seeing Mia in pain led her to the window seat and sat with his arms around her. 'Would a few euros help?' he said gently. 'The money thing is sometimes so irritating.'

'It's obvious, is it?' said Mia.

'Kelly likes people for who they are. She will like you.'

'So, she's not about money?'

'Not at all.' And he slipped a hundred euros into her pocket and went to the centre of the foyer to finish his intro.

'So, what is this object or presence the keepers of the secret hold? Maybe a stone? It's been called the third eye of Lucifer, the archangel that came to earth here and was laid in a stone cradle a few kilometres north near the frontier. It's said to be a cup the Templars held or a stone which carries a prayer. There is something here. The carrier of the secret becomes empowered. It is said sufficiently empowered to rule the world. Its local name is the "secret of ancient Girona". You know it as the Holy Grail.'

At some point that night Mia went out to cross the iron bridge and see the cathedral in the small light before dawn. There was only one question. Was he here? Two questions. Did he still . . . ? She chose the word 'care'. It was safer. A smell of wood smoke drifted up from the riverbank. It had always been for them a powerful smell associated with many of their best times. She chose to see this as a confirmation.

After a while Cynthia joined her on the bridge and said it was too late to go to bed. They watched the beginning of light in the East and felt blessed.

'I love this place.' Mia said it aloud.

'Yes, you seem as though you belong to another time,' said

34

Cynthia. 'You're sort of moving out of all this to somewhere else, better.'

'Maybe.' She hoped so.

Cynthia realized the woman looked wan and suddenly ordinary, like a ... Cynthia nearly thought 'cleaning woman'. She looked grey and too early for work and never enough sleep or enough to eat.

'This is the right place for me,' said Mia looking across at the old quarter. And now her lights came on and the nondescript 'cleaning woman' look had gone and Cynthia was relieved.

Back in the foyer the night porter made more coffee and told stories of the province.

Belle de Borromeo just lost herself in the chaos around the reception desk. It suited her. For the first time in days she could let go. Belle was a class act. They all said so. You couldn't lose that sort of breeding no matter where you ended up. And the reception girl recognized it and the night porter responded to it and they gave her the best room, kept for special occasions. She certainly wasn't a member of any group. She had found this old city by chance and this hotel was still open, lively and cheap. Just for one night. She would move onto the Ritz or its equivalent in Barcelona the next day. She took the 'superior' room because she knew her card was ok and in credit. It wasn't. It almost jumped off the machine as though electrified. Belle was unimpressed and said she'd pay later with another card. They asked for her passport. She said she'd get it later and she tipped the night porter generously and he was ready to take her luggage. No luggage. All in the car. He was happy to get it for her. She did pause before giving him the keys and then went up to the superior suite.

'She is something,' said the receptionist.

'So is the car,' said the night porter.

Chapter 6

The Rich on The Hill

*T*hree women arrive in Girona, an ancient city in North East Spain. They have never met. What do they have in common? They are getting old. What do they want? To feel young. And to keep a good face on things. 'Things' being quite a number of life issues. What do they really want? It had better be a life change or they are all in trouble. Oh yes. They are all grandmothers.

The best old fraud is Cynthia holding back 66 with both hands, who can't even handle her own liberties with the truth. Little discrepancies reappear, cleaned up and almost truthful in later conversations. Unguarded, they appear like murmurs from a nightmare. What is Cynthia? Forgetful for a start. Her voice, a touch gentle, lets strangers, especially in foreign lands, automatically trust her. She is solid from proper English stock and went to the right schools. She had been good-looking and still had the hair. But years ago, she had discovered sugar-sodden, secret comfort-eating and then she discovered you could eat anything, even your past.

Materially comfortable, middle class from the Oxford green belt, Cynthia had first married a titled landowner now on his uppers and left him ten years later for Ed, an 'entrepreneur' several years younger. Between them they had six children, seven grandchildren, a yacht, properties in Mayfair. Years ago, Cynthia had worked as a schoolteacher, a job she loved. Why did she ever give it up? She said her new young husband wanted complete attention, at least when he was actually there.

Get real, Cynthia! All the attention he needed was an absence of questions when opening the front door after an over-long business trip or closing the front door on his way to a mirage called 'the office'. He wanted the house, the sports car, the titled wife, but he needed something called 'freedom'. Cynthia, you should have stayed teaching school. Those years were the happiest of your life. You could have fitted him in. Now you are worn out by his infidelities

36

you believe no one knows about and you do more of that eating anything as long as it's enough and busying yourself with those local Women's Institute activities you don't even care for anymore. Your husband, Ed, never needed all that attention. You tried to smother him. Why? You didn't trust him. Not even from Day One. You knew those businesses were a little hard to define and even your son said he's in the rackets. So, there's Cynthia confused with her blood pressure rising, trying to diet. She wants to find her real self. She's been given the ten-day retreat in Spain as a gift from a well-meaning friend, Jenny, to resolve her failing marriage. Shouldn't she be a little more prudent and look a gift horse in the face? Old sayings are one thing. Modern-day treachery another. Come on, Cynthia! How did the well-meaning friend give you the ten days leave of absence? Yes, it's true she admires your WI work organizing the charity events, setting up the stalls for the summer fêtes. You have become a voice of female green belt. When Jenny came around, you were on your knees, literally. You wouldn't tell that to this lot in the hotel, especially the newly arrived one with the flash car. Jenny came into the kitchen supposedly on impulse but really looking for Ed, but again he's never at home. You just dropped down with the hopelessness of it all and Jenny, surprised you can even get on all fours, asked, 'Cleaning?'

'Crying,' and Cynthia reached for a cloth and started wiping the floor.

Jenny tried to sound concerned as she asked if it was true Cynthia didn't have a cleaner. Automatically Cynthia defended everything. Ed's old-fashioned, she said. He liked the old ways. Jenny got the cloth and hurled it in the bin. 'But you're not old-fashioned. Why don't you just piss off and leave him.' Jenny was one who, it seemed, knew more of the story than Cynthia would have liked. Jenny helped her up off the floor and into a chair. She made her a cup of tea and asked if she wanted to talk. Cynthia ate too many biscuits and said her husband wanted everything hand-washed.

Jenny waited. 'Surely not all the story.'

'Women look after men, darling. Even when I had the fourth baby, he said I must hand-wash the nappies. He would not agree to a washing machine. Said it made women lazy.' For a moment Cynthia sounded as though she had sacrificed for her master and like a slave was proud of it. It upset Jenny. 'He's mean.' Jenny was unaccountably angry. She knew money wouldn't be the real cause of Ed's behaviour. Maybe on the subject of his marriage there was more still alive than he admitted.

'That's what my daughter thinks. He's tight.' And that's all Cynthia would say about it.

'Look. I've got a booking for a trip to Spain and I want you to have it.'

Come on, Cynthia. That's where you should have cottoned on. Jenny, young with the tight curves Ed likes. And good old Ed, 'wealthy', youthful, always reinventing himself. This is one story you don't tell. Certainly not to these grandmothers — tough mutton dressed as lamb.

And Cynthia opened her eyes screaming. She turned in the bed sweating. 'I thought I'd been talking to my grandmother. It's unreal.' It was only too real.

Mia, 63, is trying to get over the loss of a magical career that should have continued for life. She'd had a colourful and sometimes celebrated past. Growing up in London in the late 1950s she'd loved the Bohemian artists' life of Soho. Dancing in the trad jazz clubs, meeting the poets and musicians in the all-night cafes, taking the Golden Arrow night train to Paris. She had listened to the legendary writers Jean-Paul Sartre and Simon de Beauvoir in the Cafe Bonaparte. She had met Sidney Bechet on the Right Bank and the artists in The Dome and the Rotonde. Travelling as far as the Spanish border, she met the man she never quite forgot, Sal Roca. Mia did well at art school in London and had a promising career as a painter. After her first exhibition at 21 she was established and sought after. Always seeking adventure, loving freedom, she spontaneously set off across Europe taking the roads as they came and those months were her happiest time. She married a photographer in Prague and he took her to Hollywood where she met the legendary and famous. His photos of her made him famous and she went back to painting but had lost the edge of the early successful years. She was 30 and out of date. Her husband left to work on films in Europe and she, pregnant with her first son, took a variety of jobs to keep going. She always painted, mostly at night. It made sense of her life. After several months she tried to restart her career in London and Paris but returned to LA, married a musician in a rock band, gave birth to a second son. She took up teaching art to movie stars. Most of them were too old to get roles so they turned to painting to resolve their lives.

Stop there, Mia. That's where you could have taken it further. You understood their disappointment because you felt it too. You made their creativity. Why not yours? OK, you start to hide things now. A touch of Cynthia here. She can't face the tombstone feeling inside her. Scared of the feeling of disappointment Mia has to run for it. Escape was her drug. She liked the feeling of 'free' and had to have it all the time. Hey Mia, disappointment is part of life. You couldn't take the downs. Oh, remember this. You were a good mother, solid about your children. Back to the painting for has-been movie stars. Several did well, others died from old age, ill health or career collapse. Her musician husband died of exhaustion and drugs leaving a couple of hit songs and a load of debts. His previous wife took the songs' profits and left Mia the debts. Her work got her through the tough times and she became established as a teacher to the stars. Trouble is she wanted to be a successful painter in her own right.

She was nearly 60 when younger, nubile painters started vying for her place. Hollywood always supported the cult of youth and suddenly she too was old. 'My face is my clock. Just like it is for the actors.' A has-been star teacher over 60 she came back to London, her life empty. She no longer had a partner. She'd been away too long to restart herself in the UK. Money was running out and she rented a studio and started a new life practising yoga and meditation. It worked for a while. Her two sons and three grandchildren lived in different countries. Sixty plus she felt out of place and lonely. Close friends were dying. Depression was a state unknown to her and she went for a check-up. She had always given her children freedom and encouraged them to live their own lives. She was there for them when they needed her, especially financially. Why then didn't she call them now?

What was she escaping from this time? Reality, Mia. We all play the game. On the matter of death, we live in denial all our lives. It cannot be part of our daily expectation. Unthinkable. We keep going. The clever moment is to know when denial should switch to acceptance. Hello, Death. At that age when it has to be recognized, I doff my hat to its approach as I pass into another day's portion of life. Denial has no place suddenly.

She was ill and tests were suggested. She feared the worst and during one bad night decided to go back to a place from her youth when she was happy. She'd never expected this ending. She'd spent her money generously because it would never cease. It ceased. Why didn't she call on the children? Didn't they deserve to know her true state and share it? Broke she decided to go back to Girona in Spain to the magic of long ago, to the home-town of her first love, the local charismatic political activist, Sal Roca. Suddenly he was there alive in her mind, a man she will never forget. On her deathbed he would be the one she will remember. But would he still be in the city? Or even in life? She'd last seen him, briefly, 30 years ago and helped him restore the centre of Cabala from the Middle Ages. She'd returned to Hollywood and it was said he married a local girl.

Escaping again, Mia? Wanting that feeling of freedom? You never handled things. Accumulate? You sneered at that. Save? You had the cash but you never nailed it down. Freedom has a price. You wouldn't pay the price. You could have gone on painting, put your work up yourself in a mixed show. Freedom has a price and you can see it on walls. It's called graffiti. It tells you what you need to know.

She took a cheap flight to the old city and met Cynthia who is joining a group which offered mystery, history, well-being. Mia would see what it really offered.

Belle de Borromeo, 50, the mysterious, still beautiful, femme fatale from the Côte D'Azur, is on the run from imminent trouble and in her hurried escape chances upon the unfashionable, ancient city of Girona just over the Spanish border. No one would find her here.

Belle ... real name Astrid Arup from a smart family in Oslo, the daughter of a renowned scientist and concert pianist mother. At 17 she married a university lecturer, who travelled extensively. She brought up her young son beside the Oslo fiord, swimming and sailing, skiing and skating. She loved nature. She didn't have a job and looked after her house, her son and her husband in the old-fashioned way preferred by her family. She cooked each day the traditional five o'clock main meal with homemade dumplings and seasonal food. It was unlikely her husband was the father of her son,

40

born six months after the marriage. Svelte and beautiful, Belle was ageless. After a few years she gave up cleaning house and became the party girl, the toast of society. She always felt there was more out there in life that she could not reach. Although seemingly happy there was a gnawing discontent she hid well. She was a favourite of her father, the emotionally distant professor. Her mother depended on her for support and care. Her husband had little in common with this young housewife who liked parties. She secretly had always wanted to be a psychotherapist but with her parents' attitude there was little chance of being allowed that route. She loved dancing.

Come on, Belle, that shrink thing was just an idea. You loved the outdoors, climbing mountains, sailing, taking boats along fiords out to sea. You were a tomboy. Remember the summerhouse cooking on a wood fire at the lake side, waiting for the Blue Hour just before twilight, sleeping under the stars? Mountains, hand gliding, adventure! Your best ever moment? You took a boat to the middle of the ocean, alone. It was pitch dark and there was just sea, sky, amazing stars and you sat in the darkness with just the sound of the water and gradually you understood the meaning of it all. All? Life. And don't forget that moment now. Nature. That's what you loved. You did not like the city but it gave you a monied life. A shrink, Belle? You serious? You didn't like school. You couldn't even spell. You weren't meant for a career. I hope you never forget that night on the ocean. That's who you are.

After her mother died, she looked after her father and at 28, after 11 years of marriage, left her husband for the wealthy, Wall Street-legend, Jasper Jay, 42. They met at a party. He bought her a house on the Côte D'Azur. Her leaving family and friends became the scandal of smart Oslo and she didn't go back. Her son was discreetly placed in a boarding school and her husband agreed to a quiet divorce. Jasper only loved youth and although she was 28 when they met, she let him believe she was just 17. She reinvented her past and Jasper didn't know about her son and was told only there was a young boy who was her brother, back in Norway.

For years she was the femme fatale of the Côte D'Azur, the party giver, on Jasper's money. Jasper was now obsessed by youth and she kept quiet about her age. Some said she was the femme fatale of the era. Men fell for her, young, old, rich, poor and Jasper loved it. She played her cards close to her chest and aged slowly. And then he heard rumours she had a son and to stop him foraging into her past she said he was a teenager at school in the US. Just after Belle's fiftieth birthday Jasper unexpectedly found out this eternally young son, he has never met, works for the UN and is over 30, married with a new baby. Shocked, appalled he comes to understand his mistress of many years is not 35 but over 50. She is nearly as old as him. Could it get worse? He, who could tolerate only untouched youth, was sleeping with a grandmother. He'd been duped. It was unthinkable. If he heard any more about her deception, she could end up older than even him. Jasper Jay could not bear the thought of having slept with a grandmother. He'd rather turn gay. She was out. Cheated on a deep level, he would repay her deception. How many knew about it? Was he already the laughing stock of the Riviera? He blamed the staff. Were they blind? Between a day and a night, he put the magnificent Côte D'Azur property on the market and gave his three children by an earlier marriage the rest of the property. Belle got 'bus fare' and up went the drawbridge.

The moment Belle suspected Jay knew the truth of her life she did the only thing and fast. She went straight to the bank. In her Italian sports-car she hurried to Jasper Jay's private branch in Monaco. As always, she was given premier treatment and escorted up in the private lift to the third floor where her personal manager waited to receive her. Sitting opposite each other they exchanged pleasantries but for once he did not address her as the millionaire's wife.

'Do you want your balance as usual?'

'No, I'd like my money,' she said. 'All of it.'

He didn't even hesitate. 'That would be difficult.'

A little shiver made her say, 'All my money. Now.'

Just for courtesy he checked her file and didn't answer.

'What is my balance?'

'Nil.'

She didn't believe it. 'Nil, as in nothing?'

He nodded.

The bastard had cleaned her out.

She did try for a settlement but he had cut her off. The houses, the

42

cars, the credit cards, the boat, the plane. She accused him of wasting years of her life. He replied she was a grandmother. Settlement? Look in the mirror.

Then she'd blackmail him. She knew enough of his secrets and vulnerability. Jasper's people were alerted and one who liked her warned she was not in a favourable moment. Expecting she's in danger, she took as many of Jasper's meaningful documents as she could and fled to the Spanish border. They won't expect that. Paris, yes. She hides in the first Spanish town. The bank horror has done her in. No one will look for her here. She will recover and negotiate a settlement in exchange for the proof of Jasper's dubious dealings, especially tax and political payoffs. His people will come after her for that.

An American woman in the foyer thinks she's part of a group. She decides she is part of any group. Whatever it is.

Belle had a strange night and heard a voice that seemed to be inside her. She thought it was her grandmother bucking up her spirits. The hotel waiter brought her breakfast and said it was a strange town with magical powers. Spirit voices were low on the list.

Chapter 7

Cynthia and Mia met the others in the foyer, smartly on the hour. Surprisingly The Cat was not waiting at the hotel as expected or taking breakfast at the cafe opposite. The dining room was empty except for Dick Topper enjoying a hearty breakfast of eggs, tomato and ham with a side of fried potato mashed with spring greens, Catalan style. Cynthia was drawn more to the breakfast than him and asked how he got it. She said hotels in Spain usually had that croissant and baguette thing. 'I haven't seen a spread like that south of Portsmouth harbour.'

Dick Topper, wearing a substantial sweater and walking boots, was calm and ready for only an enjoyable day. He had a map spread out and a Spanish dictionary open on the table and was planning a walk through the old quarter to the countryside beyond. 'I like the sound of Los Angeles,' he said.

'So do I,' said Cynthia and glanced at the map.

'It's a village quite high up. I rather like that,' he said. 'Just in case.'

'Well yes,' said Cynthia. 'I think we all need Plan B at this time. Do you know The Cat?'

'Not at all,' he said and poured delicious fresh coffee from a jug. She liked the look of everything on that table.

'Why don't we just eat breakfast here,' she suggested.

Mia was more concerned to establish the day.

Dick Topper called the waiter for baked apple with cinnamon.

'I know a cat has nine lives but I'm rather worried about this one,' said Cynthia. 'Is she alright? Maybe it's a Spanish thing. You know — mañana.' She watched him eating the cooked apple. 'You need cream on that. Fresh cream.'

His eyes lit up. 'You're right. I do.'

And she held his gaze quite imprudently. And in that moment, they fell in love. With food.

The group were assembled outside on the paseo deciding whether

44

to take a breakfast opposite. Lily was looking a little less sure of things. Mia was decided on someone going to Kelly Brooke's dwelling and asking if necessary, for municipal help. Lily tried not to shiver. Did Mia mean Police? Hospital? Lily went with Mia to the reception. The receptionist called the manager. Lily needed to know if there had been an incident or other violence in the area to account for the essential leader's disappearance. The manager cut through all that and sent an assistant to check out a nearby bar where The Cat sometimes stayed.

'Drink,' said Cynthia. 'That's obvious.' She indicated the manager. 'He's onto it. The Cat got too happy on her own before Happy Hour.'

'But the woman last night,' said Mia. 'The amazing one. Surely that was her?' She asked Lily how The Cat looked. Lily was beyond adjectives; she'd been up all night and hadn't slept for 30 hours. Mia told her to go to bed and she would look after the group and take them around the old quarter. 'I'll show them around the cathedral and the Cabala centre.'

Lily's voice shook with sheer exhaustion. Because she worked in admin and was an ardent follower of Kelly Brooke, she seemed to think she should be in control. 'We can't take over. We are not Kelly Brooke. We must refund everyone's money.'

The receptionist immediately cut in and said most of them hadn't yet paid any money. Dick Topper said he had paid but was easy with whatever was decided. Lily said two other participants were expected that afternoon and they should be cancelled. The receptionist said unfortunately they had paid so could not be cancelled. She also liked Mia's idea of getting the group out on a sightseeing tour. 'Let's give Kelly Brooke until 11. And if no show then you do the walk.' She gave Mia another set of keys. 'Lady Cynthia wants you to have a spare just in case...' The end of the sentence tailed off.

Lady? Surely not. The speed with which Mia doubted it surprised her. The title like the young elusive husband were somehow to be disbelieved on sight.

'So, we've got the top drawer amongst us,' said Maggie. 'You can buy titles you know.'

Yes, thought Mia. My conclusion exactly.

'What's her name?' asked Maggie.

'She's a Seymour-Coy,' said Lily.

'If she's one of those Seymours that makes a difference. Good lineage. Descended from the Tudors.' Maggie didn't sound snobbish. Just matter of fact.

Mia presented a plan for the day and the group said it was good enough.

'I've also worked in LA,' and she described a similar painting course to the one she could provide that afternoon. 'First we meditate and then paint what we have seen. In a place like this you can see more than usual. It makes the painting experience deeper.' They wanted to know about the Cabala centre. No problem there. She'd helped start it. She didn't specify how, or how much, or how little she'd done. Others wanted to know about the history.

'You've obviously been here at some point,' said Maggie unwillingly. 'You seem to know the place.'

Cynthia said she was absolutely keen on the day's programme especially the painting and how lucky to have a guide who knew the place in the past.

The group appeared grateful and would give Kelly Brooke till noon and then be ready to set off.

Relieved, Mia crossed with Cynthia to the cafe opposite for breakfast.

'There's something about all this,' said Cynthia. 'It's fishy.'

'This is a project that might fold,' said Mia. She'd seen a lot of 'folding' in her life. Then she saw a reflection of herself in the cafe mirror. 'Here's an example of "folded".' Had she always looked like this? She had certainly lost weight. Her face was gaunt. 'Do I look this old? I don't think this place suits me.' She looked closer into the mirror.

'It's the humidity,' said Cynthia. 'There are two rivers.'

'Three,' and Mia rearranged her hair.

'One thing. I don't want to go home. It took so much effort just to get here,' said Cynthia.

'I agree. And the money thing.'

'Have you paid for this?' said Cynthia.

'Not yet.'

Cynthia recalled there was mention of a money hitch the previous night. She explained a friend of hers, Jenny, had paid the fee upfront as a gift and she was more than happy to help Mia with her expenses.

Cynthia had a lovely voice which summoned up resonances and atmospheres. It was unlike any other. She had a sturdy allure which age had not quite dimmed. The touch of voluptuousness belonged to a different hormone era. By habit it still offered an undoubted but dated invitation but a response she did not encourage. Under it all she was tired. More, played out. Mia asked if she had been an actress at one time. She had not.

'What do you actually do?'

'Do?' Cynthia was surprised. Then she remembered she was talking to Mia. 'I've done absolutely nothing with my life.'

Mia recalled when Lily asked that question, she'd said crisply, 'I'm into horses.'

After the tortilla with potato and onion, manchego cheese with homemade quince marmalade and bio yoghurt with seeds, they felt a small rest by the river was required. Cynthia was hot, overwrought and out of breath. One ankle was swollen and she understood that to be a bad sign. On her side Mia had the knee problem and was limping.

'How long is this walk through the old part? Don't take it personally if I have to stop and sit under a tree,' said Cynthia.

'What happened to that beautiful dark-haired woman? Obviously not part of this group,' said Mia. 'For a moment I did think it was The Cat.'

Cynthia peeled off her jacket and the freed-up arms were surprisingly floppy. The removal of a silk undergarment released an unexpected pouch of fat on her stomach. The disciplinary clothes held everything in but were now a size too tight. 'I have to watch the eating thing a bit,' she said.

The hotel foyer was deserted. In the middle a huge pyramid of luggage, mostly built up from the extensive possessions of the two artists from Baltimore. Mia asked what was happening.

47

'They've left.' The receptionist didn't look up.

'What all of them?'

'Nearly all.'

'Where have they gone?' Mia was taken aback.

'The coast.'

'My day's plan obviously didn't appeal to them.'

'No,' agreed the receptionist, quite candid. 'Sean Penn and superstars appeal to them. You're not a big enough draw.' The girl corrected herself. 'I mean no one is, except The Cat.'

'Well, we should have a new tour. "Hunt the guide",' said Cynthia. 'Let the superstars loose on that. Is there anyone left?'

Lily, aged by a generous ten years, came out of the lift. 'There are two American women who arrived in the night.'

'Eric?'

'He's coming back. He has to arrange the delivery of their luggage.'

'Where are they?'

'A singer has taken a house for the summer. They are all there. Don't take it personally.'

'I don't,' said Mia. 'I'll leave that for The Cat. No one mentions her.'

'No,' said Lily as though talking about the dead.

'We should get the skull that knows everything to tell us where she is,' said Mia.

Eric came from the dining room. 'The skull might know but unfortunately that's with Eva and she's gone.'

And then Dick Topper came in through the swinging revolving doors, jolly and almost innocent in his pleasure. 'Come on then. Let's start on this guided walk. I've been looking forward to that.'

Chapter 8

The untidy group, knocked out by the midday heat, wound through the narrow streets and courtyards of the old quarter and stopped at the Arc Bar. It was the first cool place and Mia chose a table outside in the shadow with an overpowering view of the front of the cathedral with its 99 steps going up to the unchanged entrance. In fact, little was changed and the cathedral with its stately form, its undeniable character, demanded a deserved respect. It had made no concessions to age. There were, as Mia remembered, some curious oddities in the building and a host of unusual legends and fables handed down through the ages. It rose above the shadowed group, huge between earth and heaven and they, simple human beings, sat absorbed by its power, unspeaking. She ordered a jug of iced tea with mint and lemon and potato crisps to make up any salt depletion from the unexpected heat spike. She pointed up at the cathedral as though giving a salute and said its nave was the widest in Europe and it was considered a miracle that it could even stay up.

'I know the feeling,' said Cynthia.

'Originally a temple to Jupiter it became a modest version of a church sometime during the ninth century and was restored to its present form in the Middle Ages. It was considered unusual to build a cathedral on top of a hill.' As though in protest, its chimes reverberated across its stone kingdom and the group covered their ears. Mia assured them it always rang the hour twice so they would hear it again in four minutes.

'Kelly will be at the hotel waiting for us,' said Maggie irritated. She ordered a double gin and T and put ice on her ankles.

'There will be a storm,' Cynthia told her. 'It will get rid of this heat.'

Mia stood up and got their attention. She said powerful buildings were often constructed on the sites of previous temples or shrines because of the exceptional energy and positioning of these sites. There were several churches built where previous temples had stood in the Girona province. Often temples to Venus. Outside Girona on a high hill named Mt O there were remains of a church to the moon which had once been a temple used by a tribe existing before Neanderthal man. That story had been much debated over the years but Mt O was very old and considered sacred. There is also a ninth-century castle. She kept talking and the more she talked the more secure her position in the group as tour leader and art teacher became. Lily said Kelly Brooke had never mentioned any of that. She also told Mia she had lost two American women. They had obviously been left behind in the heat, climbing the first street, the Calle Forsa. Dick Topper thought he had seen them going into a food shop and offered to go and look for them. Had Mia seen them? Were they the travelling couple of the previous night? Lily said they were not from Kansas and had arrived at dawn and gone straight to their room.

'What do they look like?' Mia asked.

'Fat. Very overweight,' said Maggie, matter of fact.

'Oh good,' said Cynthia automatically. 'Makes me feel better.'

'They should not be out in this temperature,' said Maggie. 'You can't just take over a group. You have to look after a group.'

Mia wondered how many pairs of overweight girls did there have to be.

'I don't recall seeing more than two,' said Cynthia.

Cynthia thought she heard Maggie say, 'Looked in the mirror recently?' Cynthia, deciding it must be her imagination, ordered a Tia Maria liqueur, long version on ice. Maggie looked at her with something approaching approval.

Mia described how Jean Cocteau and Salvador Dali used to visit the Arc Bar. And Ava Gardner, Umberto Eco, the Italian writer who used the experience of living in Girona in his bestseller, *The Name of the Rose*. Cynthia remembered she had seen the film. Mia added, Luis of the Arc had helped its research. In those early days of the bar's opening Luis worked as a guide at the cathedral during the day and had taken Umberto up there at night and shown him the cathedral's secrets.

'Any other famous people?' Dick Topper was thrilled.

Liz Taylor when she was filming further down the coast. James

Mason and Melina Mercouri when they were filming *Mechanical Pianos* in Cadaques in the early 1960s. There was nowhere like the Arc Bar. They came for the jazz, the late-night atmosphere, and Luis the proprietor with his shades and eternal cigarettes, giving the up-to-date lowdown on the city.

'I'm having a hard time wondering just how Ava Gardner got herself up to this little parochial bar in this bureaucratic town of passage between France and Barcelona.' Maggie's voice had an edge. 'Are you sure you're not muddling it up with Barcelona or somewhere in the south?'

Mia breathed in and out and stayed calm as she prepared an answer. It was about then she noticed the graffiti on a stone wall. Graffiti was rare in the old quarter. She paused to make sure of what she was seeing. A demon sitting hunched on a heap of gold coins? The demon she realized had far-seeing eyes that, although they looked beyond everything, were blind. There was a long central aspect to the face that seemed to dominate and was utterly without mercy. It just existed for its own purpose. It was the face of a demonic beast. Satan? The creature wore the hood of some religious order and a cross hung on a chain below its throat. It was unearthly. Not the shape but the uncaring, completely distant formation of the face. It didn't see people. It belonged to something else altogether. She hoped, 'how she did', that this graffiti was simply made up of shadows and reflections and would fade with the change of light.

She turned away, both from Maggie's sardonic expression and the thing on the wall, and spoke quietly. Her voice was soft as it had been all those years ago when consoling the once famous actors that their lives had not ended but given them the tools for a different journey altogether, the road into adventure, image, colour, imagination. And then she recalled for one vivid moment the star of *Easy Rider*, Dennis Hopper, jumping right out of the drugs and the craziness into a cool place of form and shape he wanted again and yet again to revisit. 'Ava Gardner had been here in 1953 and stayed at the Peninsula Hotel just down on the edge of the old part when she made *Pandora and the Flying Duchman* with James Mason. They filmed on the coast at

51

Tossa de Mar. This was the place to go at night and she came back again during an affair with a bullfighter.'

'What, to this place?' Maggie couldn't scoff enough.

'To the Casa Vela on the coast near Playa de Aro. It was the celebrity spot at the beginning of the 1960s and had wonderful entertainment — Carmen Amaya the dancer, Sinatra. Ava Gardner came to the Arc Bar late in the night.' She knew Maggie was going to be trouble.

'And Taylor?' said Maggie. 'You mentioned her.'

Mia talked instead about the stones of Girona reputed to have a magnetism that drew certain people back time and again. It had to do with ley lines and at certain points the energy creating a pull and push was too strong and unusual things happened. The spirit of Girona was what mattered. It had to approve of you otherwise you passed through that old quarter and it showed you nothing. 'I believe that the spirit of the city approved of me as I was then. Of course, it would not let me go. A city's love does not die.'

She explained the area had been an Iberian trading centre dating back three thousand years. 'That's what they used to say but it's much older. The Dolmens and ritual stones testify to that. There are pieces of animal bone going back twenty-five thousand years. Before Neanderthal man there were tribes...'

'Neanderthal man?' said Maggie amused.

'The ones with long heads who did the cave paintings just across the border. I'm sure you've seen those.' And she carried on talking.

Cynthia, noticing her swelling knee, scraped forward an iron chair for her to sit on and Dick Topper said enthusiastically that she certainly knew her stuff.

'What you said about the city not letting you go,' said Lily, 'Carcassonne has the same legend.'

It would become rapidly a chatty one-upmanship competition if Mia didn't take care. She stayed standing. 'The Iberians date back four thousand years. Before that the Celts settled in clusters in the countryside because the place was warm and fruitful. Each time I come here I may be older but so is the city. The walls are now over four thousand years old and have all the scarring of past wars with the French. The civil war with Franco and the fascists in the 1930s. Girona, part of the Republic, lost and direct rule from Madrid followed. English men came and fought on the Catalonian side. George Orwell, the writer, *Homage to Catalonia*.'

Maggie ordered a double gin and offered the same to Cynthia who did hesitate but caught Lily's stern look. Did the rules still apply if the leader wasn't present? Maggie was about to cut in with another remark but Mia, still standing, pointed out various landmarks.

'Visitors always come to this province. The Greeks 2000 BC, the Phoenicians. The Jews, they were certainly here 200 AD. The land was full of minerals and tin, and good for trading. The Romans laid out the centre of the old part leading up from the river. The Moors came up from the south. Charlemagne...'

Maggie spoke up, 'I still don't get Liz Taylor.'

'You certainly know your stuff,' said Topper. 'Let's go and have lunch. On me.'

Was he talking directly to her?

'So, the Romans came?' said Maggie. 'And when did Taylor come?'

Mia talked instead of Charlemagne's arrival in the city which lasted longer and was more memorable. It was during the Moorish invasion and a sign appeared on the sky and saved the city. 'Elizabeth Taylor stayed in S'agaro on the coast in La Gavina Hotel. She stayed several times. She had been in the area while making *Suddenly Last Summer* further south with Monty Clift.' Also, she had known Sal Roca quite well. Possibly too well. So, Mia had heard.

Maggie wasn't going to let it go. 'Was she here with Fisher?'

'Many celebrities stayed in La Gavina. It was *the* spot in those days.' Times and dates were becoming unsure in the heat. She was sweating profusely, her knee resting on a chair. She sat down at last and drank mineral water. 'Celebrities came here because it was unspoiled. Truman Capote ... the king of Italy ... Sinatra....' She turned to Maggie. 'Why don't you ask at La Gavina about Taylor?' She could have added Sal Roca, the local activist, stayed there apparently with her, so rumour has it.

No rumour there. Don't be faux naive, Mia. Not your style.

'Rumours are to be respected in this area. It is active with coincidences, repeat meetings, the unexpected, the expected. Everything is more dramatic here. Something that occurred here could go unnoticed elsewhere.'

'I can begin to see that,' said Cynthia.

'I knew Taylor well.' And Maggie got to her feet. 'She can't have found much here for all these visits you mention. So, it can't have impressed her.'

Mia would have loved to reply, 'Well my old lover certainly did.' But it would not do any good. She would be watching and waiting for Mia's first mistake. And Sal Roca's dalliance with a superstar could have been cat talk in the street.

Cynthia turned to Maggie. 'Do you like this metaphysical sort of thing?'

'Not at all. I'm here because I like Eric.' And she put down a large note as her part of the bill.

Mia did not know Luis' son, the new proprietor of the Arc Bar, and that the interior had changed, but the cathedral had not. Wickedly she suggested a slow climb up the 99 steps as the interior was worth it. She knew they would say no so she was safe there. Dick Topper, however, with a happy smile said he was up for it. Today, his face was innocent like a flower. She ignored him and finished her short history without mentioning Sal Roca except as 'the activist'. She knew the city and its purpose. To be free of then-fascist Madrid.

'Surely before your time?' said Maggie.

Mia reminded her Franco didn't die until 1978.

Dick Topper was full of praise.

'Did you study here?' he asked.

'Only life.' And she suggested they walk slowly down to an old restaurant near the river for lunch. Maggie and Lily wanted to go back to the hotel because there would be at least news of when Kelly Brooke would take over.

Before they left, Mia asked Cynthia to come and look at the graffiti on the wall. Walking even worse than Mia, Cynthia hobbled across the cobbles to the barely discernible design. It didn't worry her. One look was enough.

'What is it?' Mia asked.

'A flower in a window box.'

'Are you kidding?'

Cynthia chose different lines as the principle design and Mia could see it might just possibly be something ordinary.

Don't be even more stupid, Mia. It's the moral message you should have taken in years ago.

'It's the heat,' said Cynthia. 'Let's go and eat with him. At least we've got rid of her. Why is she so nasty? Do you know her?'

'Thankfully, no.'

Eric caught up as the group set off down the eighth-century Calle Forsa street with the Cabala centre up a sloping passage to one side. He said there was no news of Kelly Brooke and started taking photographs. Maggie was disgruntled and said she would join the real group at the coast. The cobbled streets agitated Mia's knee and the bandage felt too tight. But she learned one thing on this uncomfortable walk. She could change the way she felt. Instead of sinking into the knee pain she absorbed the ever-changing scenery around her. She was filled with the outside and the inside was filled with memories. There was no space for physical pain. She talked about the entrance to the Cabala centre and how the seventh-century passage had been opened up in the 1970s. She said the door had been repainted Mediterranean blue.

'For protection,' said Eric.

The stones were healing. The past was more powerful than the present. The present moment was simply a doorway into a larger vista back then — who knew to where.

'Your knee,' said Cynthia. She, Mia, had not noticed it. She tried to get the group to think visually. To recapture the view in a short meditation, eyes closed. Cynthia was struggling inside and out. Lily was doing her best. Maggie was quiet. Eric present. Dick Topper over-enthusiastic.

'You certainly know your stuff,' he said again. From that moment on he stayed close and bombarded her with questions to which she did not give answers.

'But you must have studied here?'

She did not want any stirring up in this town of either curiosity or gossip. If she came face to face with her past so be it. The lover must never know she had come looking for him. At that moment, as she turned into the Ramblas, she came face to face with a middle-aged, sturdy woman she thought she recognized. They passed each other and before crossing out of sight Mia turned and the woman had stopped and was staring at her. There was something familiar about the eyes. Was it someone from the old days in the Arc Bar?

'I wonder if that woman from last night moved on,' said Cynthia.

For a moment she wondered what woman. 'I'd completely forgotten her.'

'Me too. How far's the restaurant?'

Before they got there a waiter, waving a tea towel, ran out of a bar and said they must help. Two ladies were in trouble. Mia looked into the narrow interior and saw a large woman lying spread out across several chairs, covered with wet towels.

'She is one of yours.'

Mia hoped not.

The waiter's mother was putting ice on the woman's wrists. Lily took over and lifted back the wet towel. It was one of theirs.

'Heat?' Mia said.

'Drink,' he said.

The other was on the floor propped against the wall. The waiter tried to explain the dilemma. They were too fat.

'I should take a picture of this and send it to my husband,' said Cynthia.

After helping to get the ladies onto a bench under trees, they did reach the old restaurant, Can Bonet, and had an enjoyable lunch.

Chapter 9

Cynthia came down from the room where, she implied, she'd received a satisfactory landline phone call from her husband and although he wanted her home, she was determined to stay. Did he ring? Did anyone ring? Mia had been in her room for almost as long as Cynthia and there were no phones ringing in that corridor. She gave it the benefit of the doubt but still said those long domestic calls always ended the same. What she meant by that she couldn't say herself but Cynthia replied it had been just that, a long call.

'You'll never guess what happened earlier. That woman is still here and she's not only staying, she's part of the group. She's called Belle.' Cynthia's face did twitch, laughter on the way.

A senior moment for Mia. 'Eva, the one with the skull?'

'The beautiful one with the black gleaming hair and that's a surprise too. It's a wig. By mistake I went into her room, the door was open. Frankly I am so tired I don't know what I'm doing but I'm beyond sleep. She was sitting at the dressing table brushing this quite short, platinum-blonde hair, back at the sides, in a sweep, like a D.A. Remember Tony Curtis and the Duck's Arse in the late '50s? Both sides swept back. And the black wig was lying on the dressing table beside her. It was like a Hitchcock film. She was looking at me in the mirror with those provocative eyes. She is beautiful but with a little something extra. The room, it's a suite, not bad.' Cynthia sat down ravaged by tiredness. 'I still can't remember the couple of fat women last night.'

'There were two outsize couples,' said Mia.

'So, I was drunk. But better than Alzheimer's.' She looked round for the waiter and asked for a vodka pickup, then she saw the clock. 'Whoops, a bit early. Make it a mineral water. You did well this morning. I think you should take over. The Cat has scarpered and this lot will just disintegrate. I can't bear the thought of going home.'

Mia agreed. At least she'd try the art class.

'No, I mean the whole thing. And you will get all the money. The hotel is in a squeeze over this missing Cat thing and you could do yourself a deal.'

Mia tried to be realistic. She didn't feel that great. A night's sleep would help. She remembered the experience of walking down from the Arc Bar and, filled by thought, she'd transcended her physical pain. She stood up. 'Let's try.'

'They're in the cafe opposite. What's left of them.'

They crossed the paseo and a scurrying wind filled with street dirt whipped their legs, lifted Cynthia's hair. Mia took her arm. 'It comes from the mountains. Sharp and sudden.' This passage was the crossroads for all weathers. Damp, bright and clear, roaring with thunder, speared by lightning, soft and sweet from the south.

Eric sat compressed between two overweight girls who were spooning up rich chocolate mousse dotted with thick cream.

'The pudding is organic,' said Eric. 'It's the best I can say about this moment. I'll pay you not to take my photo.'

As soon as Mia sat at the table Dick Topper came in and joined her. Maggie was lying down in her room. Lily prepared to greet arrivals, a doctor and his companion from Malaga. The reception was still trying to appear normal.

'So, where is she?' Mia asked.

Eric did seem just a little awkward. 'Short answer, I don't know.'

'She'd never do this to us,' said one of the girls.

'Shall we just join the others at the coast?' said her companion. They asked what Eric thought.

'The jury's out on that one.'

'I can do it,' said Mia.

One of the girls ordered a chunk of chocolate cake. 'I am not over the top, Eric, till I need to occupy an extra seat on a plane. Then "obese" comes next.' She had put Eric in his place.

The cafe conversation was drifting into the casual remarks provided by people delayed in a railway-station waiting room. The girls agreed they liked Eric's shirt and he said he was ready to take a nap. Cynthia lifted her arms in surrender and said it was a good idea but they needed to sort the group out first.

All intention would be lost, Mia could see that and stood up. It was now, this moment, she should take over. 'Let's get it on track. Go and do some yin yoga and then visit the Cabala centre as we planned. Let's start now.'

'I'd rather go to the coast.' One of the girls yawned and put her head on Eric's shoulder. It was heavy and he tried to adjust his balance without seeming to reject her.

'I've paid for this group,' said Cynthia firmly. 'And Mia is kindly offering to take us through some of the programme offered with additional experiences and some substitutes. She is a professional artist and has exhibited her work globally and taught in L.A.'

'But she's not Kelly Brooke,' said one of the girls.

'No. But Kelly Brooke is not here.' Cynthia got up. 'I'm going to do the yin yoga with Mia and visit the Cabala centre.'

'I'll second that,' and Dick Topper was up on his feet.

Cynthia looked at Eric as she would at one of her children.

'I'm in.' He got free from the lolling girl. 'You must have been a school teacher,' he told Cynthia. He turned to the girls. 'Get up and start working off that chocolate binge. The hotel has a private patio with trees. We can use that.' He took Mia's arm approvingly. 'Good on you. But reception is trying to find a replacement for Kelly.'

Mia went straight to the manager and outlined her programme. He was happy for her to spend time on the hotel premises occupying the guests but he could not be responsible or pay for her time. Cynthia quickly joined the discussion. 'What about the money that paid for my course and Dick Topper's? And the lady upstairs who arrived last night, Belle?' Cynthia reminded him of the cost of return fares from London. She had a definite authority. The manager showed Cynthia the itinerary for the next nine days and she said most of it was achievable.

'Climbing Mt Canigou? On day seven? I doubt it,' he said laughing.

'After the comfort of your rooms and your good food we can manage anything,' she replied.

'But you are not here all the time. Tomorrow you have the coach booked to take you to the spa. You return here after three nights then go with an early start, north.'

59

'We'll do it,' said Cynthia and she described Mia as a teacher who inspired Hollywood.

He started to find Cynthia amusing. Lily said other guests were arriving. Cynthia told her to go and lie down. She did look grey and drawn.

'Where is The Cat, incidentally?' Mia had taken them by surprise. They both said different things at the same time.

'Working on a vital new programme,' said Eric.

'Called away by illness,' said Lily.

'Anyone can get ill,' said the manager.

'Exactly,' Lily changed tack. 'It's getting resolved.'

The manager did like Cynthia enough to agree to free nights and meals for Mia but at the spa they would have to renegotiate.

Almost an afterthought made Mia ask where The Cat came from.

'America,' said Cynthia.

'No way,' said Eric. 'London.'

'London!'

'She will be able to relate to you two girls,' said Eric.

'I haven't got that,' said Cynthia. 'That she's English.'

'Which part? London's a big place,' said Mia.

'A place called Croydon,' said Eric.

Cynthia looked at Mia and they started laughing.

'Croydon! You can't beat it!' said Cynthia. 'You could knock me down with a feather. Croydon! She lives there?'

Eric thought so.

'It's not exactly anyone's idea of metaphysical,' said Cynthia.

'It's rough,' said Mia.

He nodded.

'So, a bit of a surprise. If you said Chelsea or Hampstead...' Mia continued.

'I wish I could,' he said.

'Where do you two come from?' asked the louder girl.

They both answered, 'London.'

The girl shrieked. 'You sound completely different.' To Cynthia she said, 'You speak posh.' And to Mia, 'Croydon.' She laughed. 'But you've been obviously in the US.'

'You sound good to me,' said Eric. 'Let's get going while they are still able to walk.'

He had changed the order and put walking first. 'The yin will only make the plump ones sleep so let's get a walk in while we can. I love this city.'

Mia explained the purpose of the Cabala centre. To restore to Girona what had once been Girona's. Jewish mysticism. She described how she'd been there from the very first moment in the early '70s. The site had been a wasteland for dogs, tramps and prostitutes. Most people had no idea it was even there. It was behind thick stone walls and had once been the Jewish centre but closed since the expulsion in 1492. Only from the house at the top of the adjoining street—which had been the palace of the renowned Jewish scholar Nachmanides, could you see the goings-on of the wasteland. And on summer nights know only too well the smells. The house owner signed permissions for the area to be restored to a centre without even reading them, he was so eager to resolve the problems. At night on the wasteland passers-by often heard the sound of digging. Neighbours nearby explained it was the ghost of the man digging for the gold of the Jews.

Mia told them the story. In part, her story and the struggle to get it accepted. She mentioned the famous helpers in Los Angeles. And Kissinger and Leonard Bernstein. She still kept Sal Roca's name vague.

Afterwards they sat in the Ramblas for a tea and she offered to answer questions.

'I have a question,' said the louder of the two girls. 'You say you come from the same place as Cynthia yet you sound completely different.'

Patiently Cynthia told her there were many different accents in England and especially London.

'And class distinctions.' Maggie had suddenly joined them and sat close to Eric. She looked at Cynthia. 'She's kept her voice and class. And Mia could come from anywhere.'

'I'm so glad,' said Mia. 'It's what I've always wanted to hear.'

'You've been to many zones,' said the loud girl. 'Yes, there's a lot of the US in your voice.'

'Does it matter?' said Eric.

'Sure. I'm used to voices and accents. I'm fascinated. Don't forget I worked in radio. Coast to Coast.'

They had all heard of that, the Big One, three-hour US prime time metaphysical radio show. Even Cynthia had heard of that.

On the way back to the hotel Mia asked Eric what he thought of the group. He looked first at Topper. 'He's one of those who, just as the coach doors close, has to get out and pee so holds up traffic, engines on, while he takes five to powder his nose. And Cynthia's one who, just when the coach actually starts moving, remembers her husband is going to call.'

'So, you've run tours?'

'Of course. I learned a lot.'

'Lesson 1?'

'Be on everyone's side. Incidentally Kay is a producer on a major TV show so good idea to keep it sweet there.'

'Kay?' There had been enough plump US girls who were seen and then gone so Mia didn't bother anymore to remember names.

Back at the hotel Lily waited with two new guests for the yin yoga session on the patio. Ramon was the Spanish doctor and his partner Gyp an accountant. They would do anything to work with Kelly and had driven all night on the off chance of getting a place. First, Lily asked Mia to list the content of her class, her positions, breathing, just to be sure.

They were all ready to start then Cynthia remembered her husband was about to call and Dick Topper had to use the toilet. Eric caught Mia's eye and winked. It was easy to laugh with Eric.

Chapter 10

Cynthia came into Mia's room and lay on the bed. 'I've gone beyond sleep. There's something going on. I can't put my finger on it but they must know where The Cat is.'

'I think your guess is right. She's off her face in some bar.'

'They're waiting for her to show up. They still think it's going to happen.'

Eric knocked on the door. 'I've got you London ladies maps.' Mia asked him in and he sat comfortably beside Cynthia on the bed. 'These maps have one purpose. They will lead you to The Grail.'

Cynthia even looked interested. 'So, it's on the map and we have to find it.'

'The map covers the area where The Grail is almost certain to be.'

'Well it will keep us occupied in case this Cat person doesn't come back and we get bored,' said Mia. 'What do you think has happened to her?'

'I don't know,' he said.

Mia did. 'I think she's shit-faced in a bar, or what if she's done this deep dimensional prep and it's sent her off the edge?'

'I think she's too good for that to happen. But I agree with the facts. She's not here.' Change of mood and he got to his feet. He suggested they all have dinner in the hotel.

No choice about that, thought Mia.

Another tap at the door and in came Belle. 'It's a little lonely in my room.' She introduced herself. Mia suggested she sit down.

'You could have joined us earlier,' said Eric immediately. 'You have come for the group?'

Belle nodded.

'Tonight, Lily will lead us in a meditation.'

'You know the hotel well?' Belle asked. Eric agreed he did. 'I wonder if you can do something to help? I've mislaid my passport and they've just phoned my room again and they need it. Can you just say I'm with you?'

'Tricky, because they need it for the police.'

Belle did gulp. 'Why?'

'The police in this country always check the register. Most hotels have a system like that, don't they? It doesn't mean anything. I'll see what I can do.' He gave Belle his full attention, his smile radiant. 'And please join us for dinner.' He blew a kiss to the grandmothers on the bed and was gone.

'He's a boy who knows how to make an exit,' said Mia.

'He's worked on himself,' said Belle. 'Trust me, he wasn't born like that.'

Mia poured glasses of mineral water and added plenty of lemon. 'Whatever he's got I'd like some of it.'

Belle was too beautiful for ordinary life. She exuded wealth. Mia had the sense that nothing much got her down. She didn't remotely resemble any of the group members or look as if the idea of 'metaphysical' meant much in her life. To fill an unwanted gap in the conversation Belle enquired about Mia's knee, then gently lifted the leg onto a pile of pillows on the bed. 'Keep it higher than your abdomen and use hot and cold compresses alternately.'

'The group isn't quite what it seems,' said Mia. 'The leader isn't here. As in "not around".'

Belle didn't seem bothered.

'Have you come a long way for this group?' Mia asked.

She did hesitate. 'A few hours' drive.' She sat on a straight-backed chair and did look sideways at the maps open on Cynthia's lap.

'Are you familiar with yoga, other dimensions and psychometry?' asked Mia.

'Definitely. So, what is the plan? Are they waiting for someone else to take over?'

Mia did not want to lose this client. Belle would make all the difference between continuing hardship and a little security. 'I will take over. Have you ever painted?' And Mia described the kind of class she had held for the Hollywood actors. She included the new aspects — meditation on the visual, and other dimensions.

Cynthia nodded approvingly.

Belle felt safer asking about her past. Mia presented only the highlights. 'And these days?' asked Belle. 'Retired?'

'God no,' said Mia, her face hot. 'I'm doing an exhibition in Cork Street, London. And I've been recently commissioned for two large countryside oils so I thought I'd do them here.'

Belle nodded approvingly. Cynthia tried not to look surprised.

'So, as the leader is a no-show, I thought I'd help out.'

'I'm so glad you have,' said Belle.

Cynthia asked where Belle lived. Belle's address near Monaco was impressive.

Be careful, Belle. This is where you learn to think before you speak. Remember your upbringing. Keeping house but out dancing and no one knew. At first.

'I sort of moved on from there.'

'Move on from that place? But there's only Rainier's palace to move onto,' said Cynthia.

Belle looked uncomfortable as though other things needed her attention. Eric rang and said Belle had to produce her passport or go to the consulate and also, they needed a credit card.

To smooth over a possibly bad moment Cynthia said travelling was such a drag these days. 'It used to be fun.'

'But we will have fun on this course,' said Mia.

How right you are, sweetie.

Belle stood up elegantly and moved Mia's knee a little to one side. 'It's got a bit of a change of colour. Have you had this before?'

Mia couldn't answer. She thought of the tests she had run from. 'I don't think I can sort of go through that right now,' and when Belle turned away Mia swallowed a couple of tranquillisers.

'I'll just go to the desk and sort out this passport business. I'm happy to do the art course with you.' She vanished from the room about as magically as Eric had.

Neither woman would have expected the silence that followed. Eventually Cynthia dragged up a comment. 'She's not what she seems.'

Nor are you! Watch it, Mia. She'll be on to your discrepancies. Don't mention that dodgy art commission again.

65

'In what way?'

'She's not come here to join a group, let alone this one. She just sort of appeared. No one knows her. I asked the hotel. Never seen her. She's got a very smart name. Montero de Valles as well as de Borromeo. And drives a Lamborghini. She starts giving opinions about what we should do. I don't know who she is.'

'I don't know who anyone is.'

'Shall I put a cold wet towel on your knee?'

That seemed a good idea. 'How old is she?' said Mia.

'I thought that would be our first question. Older than she looks. Past 40,' said Cynthia.

'She looked at me as though I could be her mother.'

'I don't know about her,' said Cynthia. 'She doesn't want to show that passport. Hiding her age? With that money I would think she had a passport that does that. Doesn't give much away.'

'I expect that woman, Maggie, will rake over her and get some truth.'

Cynthia laughed.

'What the hell do I do running this course? Other dimensions? What are these?'

Cynthia got the itinerary. 'Do just the same as they were going to do plus the art. And that yin yoga you did was very good. That fills an hour. You told it well to her.' She almost asked about the two commissioned paintings and gallery in Cork Street but said something else about painting materials and who pays for them. She started to worry about Mia. She did not believe her story of good fortune.

When she got back to her room to dress for dinner Cynthia called her son who knew these things and asked him to look up Cork Street and Mia's career. He rang back fast. 'A has-been. You need binoculars to see her last expo. My dealer thought she was dead.'

Belle asked for the manager and gave the passport with her dual citizenship and DOB that matched her years of companionship with the multimillionaire. No problem. Was she already 40? Impossible! She asked the manager under no circumstances to give her name or any details to anyone. He said a client's privacy was paramount and he would look after her personally. Bella Montero de Valles. He liked that name. There was just one tiny matter, but essential. A credit card. She said she preferred to pay cash. She was far from certain how far the bastard Jasper's influence reached and if her personal cards were compromised. Her Norwegian card she had always kept, had some few thousand kroner but the name on that card did not match the passport. The manager was happy in the circumstances with cash but needed the whole tour fee upfront. Even in her world it was extravagant and she would have to think about it. She paid for another night in the suite as he requested. The manager had hunches that usually added up to something and he'd learned over the years to have faith in them. This time he was not entirely sure but he did warn her she would need an active credit card when she reached the spa. Yes, the hunch surprised even him. This lady, for all the flounce and the names, was broke. Was this possible? Or was he going mad?

Belle sat in the corner behind a large plant but Lily still approached. 'I'm so glad you've joined us, Belle. Where are you from?' Belle needed to think quiet private thoughts and got quickly rid of the tired American intruder. She had, at most, two 'best friends' she could trust from the old days. The new 'best friends' would be on his side. He would come out with a story that would compromise her, even something against the law. Shoplifting? Forged his signature? Ten people would jump to it as witnesses. Eric thought he'd have more luck than Lily and pulled up a chair next to Belle. She answered his questions automatically wondering how best to contact the bastard she had lived with for half of her entire youth, and do a trade-off with the stolen documents and Panama affair. Also how did she raise a thousand euros? She wasn't used to dealing in such small sums. She'd get money sent Western Union from the 'old best friends' and would involve her son only if she had to. Leaving Eric in mid-sentence she went back up to the 'suite' and using her mobile, which had more adaptability than Cynthia's, reached her lawyer at home. He didn't waste time and said Jasper Jay had sent investigators out to reclaim the artwork she'd stolen from his private collection. She didn't bother to challenge the lie.

'The Pissarro?'

'The Van Gogh.'

That surprised her. 'And what am I supposed to do with that?'

'Give him back the stuff you nicked and it will look like a Van Gogh to him.'

'Do you know why I left? He got rid of me.'

'We can work on that but you arrange a place and I'll pick up the documents personally.'

She paused.

'He's got a young local guy who's sitting in custody with a story that fits with you running off with him and Van Gogh.'

'I'll go to the newspapers with the real story.'

'A matter of age difference? And a little discrepancy on your side? They'll laugh at you, Astrid.'

She hung up.

Her appetite for dinner was quite gone but to get away from that bastard was a kind of relief. Somehow these hours in this ordinary hotel had made her feel something new. She thought it was 'clean'.

Cynthia sat hunched on her bed, her head filled with the image of Mia and her damaged knee and the courage she had shown in keeping everything together. The poor broken career behind the facade made Cynthia forget even her own problems with the ruthless husband. Alone and failed but still trying. Cynthia was filled with an unusual emotion. Pity. It took away even her appetite. And the thought of Mia made her cry.

When Mia got down the stairs a woman was waiting in the foyer. It was the one she'd seen earlier in the Ramblas on the way to lunch, the one who had turned and stared with recognizable eyes. Of course, she knew the eyes. She did not remember the rest.

'You don't remember me, do you?' said the Catalan woman in English.

'Of course, I do. I just can't recall your name.'

'Mercedes Salvat.'

'A teacher?' Mia hugged her and hoped their mutual past was friendly. Of course, Mercedes was the widow of Luis. Mia did not ask about Sal Roca.

Cynthia met Belle in the corridor, as the Beautiful One, wig a touch askew, was going light-footed to the back stairs carrying what looked like her overnight bag. 'Oh, you're not leaving,' said Cynthia. 'Please don't go.' She was thinking about Mia.

'My mind isn't quite on other dimensions to be honest.'

'Nor is mine,' said Cynthia.

Belle then saw Cynthia had been crying and reached out a hand in sympathy. 'Can I help?'

'Yes,' said Cynthia. And they decided to sit in Cynthia's room and have a private talk.

On hearing of Mia's dilemma, no money, no career, family absent, she said, 'It could happen to anyone.' Her words really came from her heart.

'I really need to stay here right now,' said Cynthia. 'One or two things at home. You know how it is.'

'Not really,' said Belle. 'My life is really quite ordinary.'

Cynthia looking at the svelte luggage on the way to a back-stairs exit and a slightly crooked wig, doubted that. She reached across and deftly adjusted the wig. Belle looked at her, as Cynthia said later 'with a knowing look'. They both knew where they were.

'So, let's get this group off the ground.'

'Definitely,' said Belle. She had just realized, in her case, being with others was better than alone.

'It just takes stamina,' said Cynthia.

'And ideas and enough punters,' said Belle.

They were cheered up enough to go down to dinner. Only Dick Topper was eating. 'He knows how to choose his food,' said Cynthia admiringly.

Mia joined them and said she'd met a woman from years ago who knew the secrets of the city. And also taught physical upkeep. Running, rock climbing, the lot. 'She will do it for us.'

Hopeful they went out into the beautiful evening and drank a Ratifia or two.

Every time the phone rang in reception Mia thought it was The Cat. Lily was still upright and seemingly conscious as she changed again the room of a discontented arrival. Sitting at a table in the paseo drinking coffee, watching the locals taking their evening walk, Mia felt she was in the most right place in the world and it could not get any more right.

'Does anyone know what The Cat is supposed to look like?' said Cynthia, just to make conversation. She didn't really want to know.

'She's amazing,' said Lily, her voice dull.

'I know what she's supposed to be. I need to know how she's supposed to look.'

'Unique. There's no one like her'.

'Oh Jesus!' Cynthia went to reception and came back with facts. 'Medium height, dark hair, good body, good way of moving, slight, good attitude. Facts! Mid-thirties, travels.' She ordered another Ratafia on ice. 'No one knows where she is and she has never done this before.'

'Here's another fact,' said Lily. 'The coach ordered for tomorrow has to be paid for. It's booked to take us to the spa at 10 a.m. It seats 30 and costs 150 euros including a visit to the Dolmens at Romanyà. Facts! We should be 30. We are not 30. We are at most eight if Doctor Ramon and Gyp, his friend, decide to come.' She looked at Mia. 'You said you want to take over.'

'Yes, we'll take over,' said Cynthia.

'Then you need to pay the 150 euros upfront to reception.'

For some reason Lily, Cynthia and Mia looked at Belle who stared into a distance of different wigs, changeable lenses, a string of ever-changing names and professions. She decided she'd slip out during the night and go back to the old summerhouse in Norway. No one would look for her there.

'Let's get the money from the people boarding the coach,' said Cynthia.

'Not possible,' said Lily. 'It's included in the price of the tour but because we have so few left and most of those haven't now paid up the full amount, you, the organiser, will have to cover it.'

'And reclaim it later?' said Mia.

'When everyone feels happy enough to pay up. Catch 22. And there is one. You only lead the group for as long as Kelly Brooke is absent, then she takes over.'

'Let's get a smaller coach and cut the Dolmen trip,' said Mia.

'It's already booked. And Maggie certainly wants to go to the Dolmens.'

'Does she now? Then let her pay.' She sat silent considering the options. Then she turned to Lily. 'Why don't you take it on?'

Lily, almost embarrassed, did not expect that. 'I really couldn't. It's better a stranger...'

'Well, this stranger is not paying 150 euros for a coach with 20 empty seats.'

Alarmed now, Lily said it was the only expense to be met by the group leader. By the time they got onto the coach again, after three days at the spa, those who were still keen would have paid up the full amount for the journey north. She would reclaim her money. She nearly added, but Mia would have to work for it.

'Are you coming?' said Mia.

'I don't know.'

Ramon, the doctor, joined the women. 'What's the view on booze?' he asked Lily.

'I've no idea. Anymore. You better ask Mia.'

She told him she would take over the group and he and his friend were welcome. 'No alcohol when we're doing the practices and meditation or the artwork.'

'Painting you mean? I'm no good at that.' And he poured a round of Ratafia.

She described how it was part of a meditation practice. 'People say they can't draw or paint or they can't sing. It's not about being good but getting the right result.'

He poured more Ratafia. 'This stuff is harmless.'

It looked innocent. They gave it to babies. It could be medicinal. It was a killer. Belle got its measure but she still emptied her glass fast. What if Jasper didn't just want the documents back? But more. He would want revenge. He'd been duped. Where had he hidden the 'stolen' Van Gogh? A dozen places.

'So, we drink wine at dinner,' said Mia. The church bells chimed eleven and everyone agreed it was a delightful evening.

The sound of footsteps coming around the corner made them all look up with expectation. These were meaningful arrivals. And then they arrived, three of them, the most powerful one first. He was a well-muscled man in his forties with penetrating eyes. He was effective, professional, attractive, hard. His eyes met Belle's as he crossed between the tables, just one look. It was enough. He was followed by two men moving in an alert manner, ready for what came next. Plain clothes cops. Ramon got it immediately and Belle, after registering his undoubted attraction, realized it too. With a clap and a shout of greeting the men arrived at reception. Belle's face became bloodless, haggard, she looked ten years older. She was sweating and reached for the bottle. She took a drink in one go. Too late to hide. Of course, he'd come for her. And with one look he'd made her. Did Jasper Jay come around the corner next? Ramon poured Belle another drink and held the glass to her lips. By now she was shaking.

'It's the heat,' said Lily. It was a cool night.

'The journey,' said Cynthia.

Belle wanted to get up and walk away. Her legs didn't make it. A quick furtive glance at the men at reception. They seemed to be studying a document.

'They're here for something else,' Ramon told her softly. 'He didn't even look at you.'

But he had. Belle wouldn't forget *that* look.

Lily poured her mineral water and Ramon held her hand. Mia said she would go in and find out what it was about. It had all the appearance of a raid. Before she'd circled out of the revolving door the chief cop came out onto the paseo and stopped by the table. He was sure of himself, every movement showing his power.

'Are you part of Kelly Brooke's group?' His voice was deep and expressive.

Ramon agreed in Spanish they were.

In English the cop asked if they had seen Kelly Brooke. Had anyone spoken to her? Mia looked at Lily who, no longer decisive, said Ms Brooke had left.

Belle turned away ever so slightly which only drew his attention.

'He's looking for Kelly Brooke,' Ramon told her softly, then offered the cop a drink. The man shook his head just once sharply and again his eyes met Belle's. Perhaps as a diversion he picked up the map on the table of the Grail route they were supposed to follow. 'What's this?' He laughed and put it back on the table. 'Girona in Roman times? Nice try.' He walked away and his men followed.

'So, all he wanted was to track down Kelly. And he scared us all to death.' Cynthia did not look at Belle.

Ramon was cheerful. 'As Kelly would say, "Keep it in the moment, and every moment new".'

'If only,' said Belle and had another shot of Ratafia.

Dick Topper approached after a long evening walk. 'He looks so much better,' said Cynthia. 'This place suits him.'

'I think we should try and keep it going,' said Belle surprisingly.

'Great,' said Mia. 'How? That 30-seater coach?'

'Let's just slim it down and get a smaller one.'

'So, you're in?'

'Certainly.' All varieties of escape long gone.

As they walked to the lift Mia told her everything was alright and the cop had just come to enquire about Kelly Brooke.

Belle paused and decided to trust this woman. 'No. He came for me.'

Chapter 11

Only when they curved around the road out of Girona, north, did Mia notice what looked like a hamlet on top of a high hill off in the distance. The hill was more a small mountain and the hamlet, a castle or monastery. There were in fact several buildings up there. Then the coach swung off to Romanyà and the hill was lost. She asked Lily what it was but she had no idea.

'It was too high up,' said Belle. 'Maybe a hotel?'

'I don't remember it from before.' Mia asked the driver and he asked what she was talking about.

'The hill back there with the settlement on top and something like a castle.'

'But it was a castle. With caves underneath where the fighters for Catalan Independence were held as prisoners after the Civil War in the 1930s. The war with Franco and the fascists. It doesn't matter how much money's up there. It doesn't have a good omen that place.'

'What is it now?'

'Paradise. That's what they say. Ballroom, artworks, concerts, haute cuisine. There are said to be air lifts that take you up so fast you are level with Venus, so they say. It doesn't belong to this earth, if you ask me.'

Mia asked if he went up there.

'Not my kind. Not many from Girona are welcome.'

'What's it called?'

'The Rich on Top of the Hill.'

'Who owns it?'

'Same answer.'

'A local Catalan,' said Eric. 'So, I'm told.'

Because the coach had been late leaving Girona, the driver charged waiting time. Firstly, Maggie had to be 'persuaded' to get on it at all and Fatima, a new girl, had lost her luggage. The driver assured Mia he would have to also charge extra for the hour's wait at the Dolmens. Mia took control and cancelled the Dolmens which led to a heated discussion with Maggie. Maggie needed to rediscover the magic she thought she had located on a previous visit. Mia said as they were only six, they could take a taxi in the cool of the evening. It would also be cheaper. Eric suggested they reach the Dolmens destination and he and Maggie would get off and stay there alone and a taxi would come for them in time for lunch.

'We do the visit in the evening,' said Mia. Her determination made an enemy of Maggie but got an amused response from Eric.

Maggie asked the driver to stop while she turned for support from Lily but she was lifeless in the corner of her seat dealing with her own disappointment and did not speak. The driver said the ride was becoming crazy. What did the English woman want to do?

'The spa.'

And the driver waited for traffic to pass then turned the vehicle back towards Caldes de Marvella. 'You need to be in control running this group,' he said.

How right his words. Seeds he had sown. Which Mia would have to reap?

The rooms of the spa were old, clean and identical so there were no issues about someone getting a better one than someone else. Ramon had driven Fatima and they were in the bar. Dick Topper was making his own way. Mia, Cynthia, Belle, Lily, Eric and Maggie carried their luggage from the coach and Maggie booked the driver for the journey to the Dolmens at 5 o'clock. Eric winked just once at Mia and later said, 'Let her just get on with it. She is a feral enemy. Don't go there.'

Mia asked the group to start with a stretching and strengthening body session in the cool under the trees, a technique she'd followed daily in Hollywood. Next came breathing techniques, yin yoga, more muscle toning in the sulphur water pool. After a healthy lunch and a gentle Feldenkrais movement class she introduced a little-known technique, 'breathing the balloon', a calming visualization she'd learned in South America. The group liked that one.

During the free time before the Dolmens visit, Belle joined her in the bedroom. 'We have to kick start our lives,' she said.

75

'What had you in mind?' Cynthia came out of the shower wrapped in a towel. She could see Belle taking in the unexpected immensity of her body, its generous voluptuous bulging and sometimes flopping flesh that no everyday towel could hide. In turn Belle's eyes could hide a lot but not shock. Cynthia stepped back quickly into the bathroom.

'We have to go backwards like some of the old Jewish clocks in Girona and be young again,' said Mia.

'Better than that,' said Belle. 'A new version of everything we've learned and been through. Let's be light and free, free as birds.'

'How?' said Cynthia.

'We've got to exercise, eat a sugar-free alkaline diet, spring clean our lives, heal our resentments, seek the spiritual, defy gravity. Renew! Be new!'

'But what about the metaphysical hunt for the Grail?' said Mia.

'Oh, forget all that.' Belle couldn't dismiss it enough.

'That's what they're here for,' Mia insisted. 'We follow the Grail path with them.'

'Forget them. We've got to do something for us. Let's start.'

But Mia, only half limping today, hurried down to the group in the sulphur pool.

Belle waited while Cynthia dressed discreetly behind the bathroom door, and when she came out said, 'Why don't we all share in here together? It's cosy.' Belle desperately needed company these days. Three were better in a room than one when the cop came knocking. Cynthia supposed it was a joke. Then Belle asked if she could borrow her phone. 'I need to make a call. Mine doesn't work, for some reason.'

'Of course.' Cynthia handed her the mobile. 'Still not good coverage I'm afraid. It's better by the pool.'

As Belle went out Cynthia said to herself, 'I don't trust her.'

Belle asked her lawyer to meet her in Aix. She had switched the phone to withheld number.

'Too near to the scene of the crime,' he said.

She asked how things were.

'Full on. He's looking for you.'

Whose side was the lawyer on?

'I see you're on another number.' Disguised numbers were no problem for him. 'Is this English phone the one you want me to call from now on?'

'Will you meet me in Paris?'

'Tell me where you are now and I'll come there.'

She didn't trust him. There was a lot of distrust in the air. Jasper Jay could buy him. She couldn't even charm him enough to keep his waning legal integrity.

'It's not so much about documents. He wants me ruined, doesn't he?'

'Age is a funny thing. Some people find it wonderful. Others are others. Let's face it. Most men these days are gay or like very young girls.'

She walked around the grounds. Cynthia was the one to cling to. The lawyer called her back as she knew he would. 'I'll do a deal with Jasper. Expect household money but you have to sign a non-disclosure agreement.'

'Where is he? Having a facelift?'

'You put in some good years with him, Astrid. He owes you that.'

Belle swam in the larger pool and the water was fresh and clean. She had no plan but felt instinctively that out of the two women Cynthia was the one to concentrate on. Belle could hide somewhere in Cynthia's life which would be large and spread out and there was money around and more than two cars in that garage. Cynthia had property, of that she was sure. The other looked as though she had been something once but got lost in a lot of bad luck. She'd been alone a long time.

Through the trees of Romanyà de la Selva the group could see an arrangement of huge stones and Maggie, in the first happy moment Mia had seen, ran joyfully towards them.

'They're on a level with Stonehenge,' said Eric.

'What is a Dolmen?' Fatima asked.

'An ancient ritual stone,' said Mia. It was the best she could do.

'A Dolmen is a collective megalithic burial enclosure made up of several chambers,' said Maggie sharply.

'My! Look who's been to school!' said Belle.

Mia looked down along a covered passage also made of stone leading to an uncovered enclosure. In front of the entrance were large stones standing in a circle. 'So, what is this exactly?' Fatima asked Mia.

Mia, completely at a loss, said it was thousands of years old. She caught the exchange of looks between Maggie and Eric and decided not to go further into the unknown. 'I'm going to get this wrong,' she whispered to Cynthia.

'Get them to say what they think.'

Mia turned to Eric and asked if he would like to explain the arrangement of the stones. She made it sound as though her asking him was a privilege.

'The group leader usually knows these things,' said Maggie.

'I am familiar with standing stones or menhirs further north but I don't know this site,' Mia replied.

Maggie told her to look at the map she had been given. It was marked on that.

Eric pointed to the passage. 'The access corridor to the burial chamber is covered by thick mounds of earth and stone. This was constructed by a human group. Possibly Druids, but how?'

'Like Stonehenge,' said Fatima.

'Equally mysterious. The slabs are granite but from where did they get them? And how did they get them here? They are huge and heavy. This is built with skill. The circle of stones is for the ritual ceremony. The entrance faces south-east so that sunlight can reach the funereal chamber at the exact moments of the summer and winter solstice. Which shows that those beings followed a religious practice.'

'Thank God for Eric,' said Maggie and began to sing a strange broken lullaby.

Dick Topper asked when the Dolmen was built.

'2200 BC,' said Eric.

'So, they were intelligent beings?'

'Certainly. They were initiated beings.'

Cynthia slumped onto a stone and took off her shoes. 'I've had it,' she admitted.

Mia stood up, a position she chose when trying to address the group. 'I think this is a good place for psychometry so would you all choose stones or pieces of rock or branches from the area? Whatever attracts you.'

Maggie's lullaby faltered. 'I can sense the spirit is here, Eric.'

He was taking photographs, mostly of Mia, and did not respond.

'Eric, come here!' Maggie shouted. 'Or you will miss it. It's female. I can see her.'

Eric told Mia to stand quickly by a tree. She thought it was part of a seance. It was to take another photograph.

'You have lovely bones. I bet you've been photographed plenty in the past. The camera sort of loves you.'

Maggie's mouth opened ready to scream and Eric jumped across the burial passage, and embraced her sufficiently.

'It's a woman carrying her baby to be placed here. Eric, I saw her clearly. She's naked except for some leather strip just across her navel. But she's gone. Because the energies are not right here. There are too many wrong people present.'

Eric soothed her and promised the runaway spirit would come back.

'You've made the contact, it's fabulous. Just sing to her again and she will come.'

'It was her. I located her the last time I was here. I told you something marvellous was around these stones. And now you've missed it. Because you soil yourself with these modern-day unworthy attractions. How can *that one's* bones compare with those of an ancient being?'

Eric did his best to soothe her and so shut her up.

'I hope he gets well paid for all this crap,' said Belle.

Dick Topper obediently laid down his pieces of stone at Mia's feet. 'What do we do?'

Mia gave him the basic process of psychometry. 'Pick up one piece, hold it in your hand, see what comes into your mind. The first thought. Receive it then quickly put down the object.' She had learned this at a movie star's home in Bel Air. He did it too quickly. She told him again to hold the object, receive the first thought, then put the object down. 'What was the thought?'

Dick Topper did as she said. 'The stones seemed to go hot and, in my mind, I saw a horse. Just the front of it. Very large.'

Cynthia did do her very best not to laugh but her laughter was fatal.

'Let me try,' said Fatima. 'God, it's wonderful. I held the piece of tree bark and saw a fairy. Quite clearly.'

'Oh Jesus. You just saw Eric.' Belle couldn't laugh enough.

'Yeah that's great,' said Mia. Time to change the subject. Maggie started the croaking singing. Lily then burst into tears.

Everyone stopped. Eric jumped across the passageway yet again and used his most successful embrace. 'What is it, darling?'

'It's the atmosphere of the place,' said Maggie.

Lily shook her head desperately. 'I so miss Kelly.'

As they left the site Mia turned back. She found the arrangement of stones moving, sweet, sad. They were pure.

'I don't want to be a killjoy,' said Cynthia. 'But art class comes next and we have no brushes or paper and there's no art shop in this village. And who pays for it?'

'We'll use paper and pencils from reception and sketch a bottle of water and include meditation so they go deeper. And then they sign in for tomorrow's two-hour class.' Mia laid out an arrangement of bottles that caught the light of the pool.

Ramon joined Topper and Cynthia. They waited for Maggie but she didn't come down.

'Do you mind if I have a stiff drink?' said Cynthia. 'I'm all in.' Then Belle came barefoot across the grass with two bottles of local wine and some olives and crisps.

It was the Blue Hour just before twilight. Mia gave an introduction, spoke of her work in the past. They were more interested in the names of the movie stars she had taught than the sketching of a bottle. Even Maggie through her open shutters called down for more gossip. Hollywood painting and more bottles of wine was Mia's first success.

80

Chapter 12

'Belle has been up all night,' said Cynthia. 'I've been up since four and she was walking out there through the trees. Something's not right there. Shall I ask her?'

Mia sat up and looked immediately at the clock. 'Is it Thursday? It's when they decide. The Cat's deadline.' She drank the gently sparkling mineral water.

Belle brought in a tray of coffee and croissants. Cynthia asked if there was anything she could do.

'Do?' said Belle.

'To help. If that's why you can't sleep.'

'I like the dawn, the sun coming up. I could try and paint something like that.' She sounded calm. 'I get the feeling this Cat person isn't coming so you take over.'

Mia closed her eyes. Impossible.

'When you greet the group treat them like guests at your tea party. Dispense a few words here, advice there and refer to what they said yesterday. And get the rest of us to agree that a particular person is looking a lot better. Slimmer, brighter, as they should be, as they are going to be.'

'Group?' said Mia. 'But there's only six.'

'Talk about Hollywood.'

'I agree,' said Cynthia. 'I must say I feel better for that coffee.'

'I'll ring for some more. They are just squeezing the oranges, blending juice. Day 1, plenty of clearing foods.'

Cynthia sighed. 'I don't think I can get down there for that early whatever it is. I feel worn out. Aching all over. Did far too much yesterday.'

'Of course, you can do it.' Belle assured her that Day 2 is always tricky at the start. 'Come on, let's breathe into the balloon. Which colour today? And I will pay you but on a daily basis, Mia.' And she placed an envelope of money on the bed. 'And the new girl, Fatima, I recognize. She comes from a monied family in Dubai. Well, they all have money there. She loves the metaphysical so ask her for a fee upfront.'

They were all waiting in an obedient circle as Mia approached, smiling.

'You walk better,' said Eric. Not able to avoid Ramon's glance he stopped all cheer-up medical hype. She did not walk better. She just seemed lighter.

The group moved into the second stage of Feldenkrais and then began the Ohm chanting followed by a reflex practice and balancing.

'I do feel better,' said Maggie.

'I wish I did.' Cynthia spoke quietly. Then they noticed Lily didn't speak any more. She was just there.

Break for coffee, served in the morning sun and Mia remembered the pretty girl from the first evening. 'Isn't she one of the travelling couple? The one who read Kerouac? Where are they?'

Cynthia had no idea.

'I can't recall her name.'

'Ask Lily. At least you can try. I want to do the art classes but I'll pay you for the rest as well. I slipped something into your bag.'

Mia squeezed her hand.

'I wish I could get the hang of Belle.'

'She's not a grandmother,' said Mia.

'Is that it?' Cynthia was satisfied.

Mia noticed she didn't mention her husband anymore. Mia had forgotten his name as well.

Mia saw Eric running down the back stairs. She said, 'There are a lot of back-stair entrances and exits in this story. Where are you going?'

'Girona.'

'To look for Kelly Brooke?'

'It's Thursday,' he said. 'All yours. No-show Cat so you get the group. Whatever you do don't get their names wrong.'

'But the fat ones all look the same.'

'Because you're not looking. Yet you're an artist.'

'I was.'

'You can't lose it, Mia. And they are not fat. Only attractively plump. Cherubic. Remember, unconditional love.' He carried on down the stairs. She knew he was going to look for The Cat. To see if she was alright.

Just before the drawing class with notebooks and pencils provided by Cynthia, she asked Lily what she should charge.

'You used to hold classes in LA. Base it on that. No one in this group is broke.'

If only she knew.

Mia touched her arm. It was a brave gesture as Lily was not only down but hostile. The touch was her way of saying sorry.

Esmee Pont arrived just before the dessert of baked apple and cinnamon. She was tanned, bright eyed, wearing simple shorts and top. The green bow still bobbed gaily in her hair.

'I am here. I never left. I just took a little adventure at the coast.'

'Were Sean and Bibbi there?' asked Maggie.

'They were all there. But I went up the coast to a more authentic atmosphere. The fishing village.'

The spa had strict eating hours and she had missed lunch. The waitress told her the chef had left.

'Ridiculous,' said Esmee. 'I've known Carlos for years. He never leaves.' She went straight into the kitchen and was quickly served hot food by Carlos in person. He then presented her with a special dessert menu to follow.

'We're on a sugar-free eating plan,' said Mia.

'Ridiculous!' She called Carlos and said she'd have a bit of everything. 'Shall I sit at another table?' she asked Mia. 'Out of sight?'

Mia looked at Lily for support. Nothing doing.

Eric came back from Girona with paints, canvas and charcoal for everyone. He refused any payment as he had got it at a good price from the art shop in the old quarter. He had also brought Mia a clock with hands ticking backwards.

'Are the police still looking for The Cat?' asked Cynthia.

'If they were, they wouldn't tell me.'

'Any news?' said Cynthia.

'No news.'

'What is the hotel doing?'

Mia watched Lily blanch under her tan and it occurred to her only then that Lily must know where The Cat was. Probably spoke to her. Was she like Belle and maybe others, hiding out?

Mia stood up and asked the group to follow her outside for the workshop. They were not waiting for the French singer who could guzzle all the delicious cakes she wanted. But she would have to pay the price. Mia decided it should be 100 euros daily from each group member whether they did the whole course or only the art class. Reception had agreed to give a reduction on the room and meals. She thought the best time to discuss this was in the cooler hour before the communal walk at seven but Dick Topper brought up the subject before the canvasses were shared out.

Mia said, 'Let's try concentrating on horizons. From this garden we see two. Let them help us to really look at Horizon. What is it? Paint it. Let's try.' And she picked up her brush.

Dick Topper spoke up. 'I'd like to suggest, if I may, that we all pay something for your time and generosity.' Mia said she would discuss it later. He looked uneasy.

'What's wrong with now?' said Cynthia. 'This is our second day here and we had one full day in Girona.'

Maggie was looking at Belle. 'You don't look like someone who is part of a group. Do you know Sean Penn?'

Belle did not answer.

'I expect Mademoiselle Jolie suggested this. She's a fan of Kelly Brooke.'

Mia cut in and told them the price. '100 euros for everything we do. Also, you get a small discount on room and food from the spa.'

'100 euros? On top of what we've already paid?' said Maggie. She put down her brush.

'100 euros! That's a lot, 'said Fatima. 'For a week.'

'100 a day,' said Mia sharply.

They simply looked at each other. Nobody spoke.

Finally, Eric opened his arms wide. 'I'm on as a helper. I put it together for the. . . .' He nearly said 'Cat'. 'And I do all the visuals.'

Mia's attention switched to Lily. 'I've looked after the bookings and the clients.'

Dick Topper became highly coloured and angry. 'I say, this is rotten. I'll pay now.' And he placed 500 euros on the grass in front of Mia.

'I'll pay,' said Belle and winked at Mia.

'And me,' said Cynthia. 'Glad to.'

Esmee joined them with a plate of cake and a small coffee. 'Is this psycho-drama therapy?'

No one answered.

'I love it. I can see by your faces it's going deep. I will join in.'

Fatima reached out and took a chunk of the cake, before Eric could stop her.

'It will cost you a hundred a day, Esmee,' said Maggie.

'How do I answer?' said Esmee laughing. 'Don't be ridiculous!' And then she realized that maybe she should take the 'psycho' out and just leave the drama.

Ramon cleared his throat. 'Will you all hate me if I offer to pay for the art class and that only. So, when I'm present, I pay whatever you suggest.' He looked straight at Mia.

'It's very ad hoc,' said Maggie.

'Well it is,' said Ramon. 'That's exactly what it is.'

Mia sat very still, composed, allowing them just enough time but no more. She had done the same in the Dennis Hopper days. Whatever, I must not cry, she thought.

'Look I hate being in this position,' Ramon said. 'I drive all this way from the south to get an experience that I value but it is not on. I've quarrelled with my partner who has left to have a jolly time in the clubs at the coast. I don't think it's right to be asked for money like this.'

Dick Topper ran hollering furious out of the gate.

'Let's start.' And Mia picked up her brush.

The group produced a variety of styles from tiny smudged designs full of the fear of failure, to childish rebellion, to carmine red 'disobedient angry'. None of it had to do with the proposed subject. Only Belle produced a glittering yellow strip of a horizon at dawn which she enjoyed painting. However, they did transform their stress and hostility into concentrated activity and they discovered something else. By using their creative result as a focusing tool they could, with eyes closed, let its imprint take them on a journey of shapes and vistas, of sensations and anticipation, to another state of being.

'Let this, what you've produced, be your mantra,' Mia said.

'If I'd known it was going to be used like this, I would have done something better,' said Ramon.

'Use it as a incredible travelling tool or as a key to unlock one of the padlocks of the not known.'

'You should have explained what you wanted.' Ramon was angry. 'You don't give the full picture. If you want a result on paper that will transport us to another state of feeling then say so.'

Quite gently she told him that his intention indeed would have been different but would not have the same result. 'Another time, another picture. The horizon is a good talisman because it takes you to where you can reach the unknown. From the known to the not seen. Let's just visualize shapes for a moment.' And she asked them to close their eyes, let go of tension, breathe fully, bringing into the mind a large red ball. 'Let it dissolve. Now see a whirling hoop of bright yellow. Let it whirl away into the distance and now approach the deep green triangle. Let it fill your thought.'

Her voice was steady and calm as she continued through a line of shapes whirling or stationary and asked them to see which one suited them. Most liked the pale-blue cube. Dick Topper chose the falling triangles of silver. The group, in spite of themselves, found the process hypnotic and Cynthia went further into sleep. The church clock tolled seven. A breeze shivered through the trees. They had been painting with breaks of meditation for three hours. Mia asked the group if the process had brought changes into their consciousness.

'Not really,' said Maggie too quickly. 'This sort of thing doesn't work for me.'

Mia managed to drag her eyes from 'the bitch who now looked like a spiteful green triangle' to the plump Fatima who had been 'misunderstood all her life'.

'You want me to say what I felt?' the girl asked.

86

'Definitely.'

'Probably not enough. I'd like to do it again.'

Ramon cut through it all and stood up. 'Whether I feel this way or that way won't happen anyway. I don't think any of this has a proven result.'

Maggie laughed. 'What's that?'

'I like things evidence based.'

'You would,' she said. 'But whatever it's done it's made you angry.'

Mia stood up and invited Ramon to sit down. She gave them suggestions for assessing line and composition. She mentioned artists past and present whose work was useful as a creative meditative tool and others whose work was not. She was at all times focused and calm. She did her work well and knew it. The group in turn waited for the reaction they were sure would come. Each one separately planned how to respond to her forthcoming attack about the with-holding of fees. And this concern, said Ramon later, affected what they produced on paper and canvas.

She brought the session to a close and they were surprised how long they had been sitting in the calm garden. She told them how to transport their canvases back to their rooms and quickly folded her easel and materials onto a neat trunk on wheels.

Dick Topper, who had returned at some point during the session, said he was surprised he could do something like painting and for so long. Mia thanked the group and pulling the small trunk walked away into the building. The group lost no time having a heated disagreement.

'How can you treat someone so badly?' Cynthia looked from Maggie to Lily to Ramon. 'I find you self-centred and hostile. And I don't want to be in your company, frankly.' She said more and later realized it was words she should have hurled at her husband years ago.

'I don't much like your company,' said Lily. 'You drink so much no wonder you're touchy.'

'I don't think drink is a subject any of us should go too far into,' said Eric quickly.

'I am surprised at least by your reaction.' Dick Topper seemed to be addressing Ramon who lost no time attacking Topper's smarmy niceness. 'You're still a schoolboy. Yes, sir, three bags full, sir. Grow up.' Underneath this dope was probably a serial killer for all Ramon knew.

Eric got in the path of the two men in case more developed. Esmee was thrilled. 'This art class has certainly produced some drama,' she said.

Eric laughed. 'I wonder what she could do with a drama workshop. Worth a try.'

'Try paying for it before you suggest that,' said Cynthia.

Belle took her arm and picked up her canvas which Cynthia snatched back and tore to pieces. The group loved it.

Esmee laughed. 'It's even better than I thought.'

'If Kelly was here this would not have happened,' said Lily.

A sudden silence it seemed no one could handle.

'It's Kelly's fault,' said Maggie eventually. 'She isn't here. She's let you down. Accept it. Or get angry. You don't have to make yourself ill.'

'Be angry, Lily.' Eric took her in his arms. 'We can take your pain.'

Belle picked up the particles of Cynthia's canvas and got her away to safety.

Maggie got to her feet. 'Let's all go and have a drink.'

Upstairs Mia sat slumped in silence. I will never ever ask them for one dime, she promised herself. And even better she would never accept one buck if they should think twice about paying her.

Cynthia brought in the biscuits. 'There's nothing like a good cup of tea.'

Belle looked out into the garden. 'They're still arguing.'

'Maybe that's what's meant to happen,' said Cynthia. 'Clears the air.'

'There is something about the energies of the place,' said Belle. 'And this spa is included on that "find the treasure" map. Who thought that one up?'

'Just a trick for a rainy day,' said Cynthia.

Then Belle and Cynthia told Mia how well the class had gone. Belle said she had had a real experience and something was processed inside her. 'I'm grateful.'

There was quite a long silence and Cynthia did not know what to say and Mia had nothing to say.

'I should have said more,' said Cynthia. 'It's my fault.'

'Oh, please don't,' said Belle. 'That's taking it on yourself. Never do that.'

Cynthia ripped fingers through her hair wrecking any style that could have been there and considered going home. This was too much. It had turned into some kind of dodgy therapy. Of course, she always did that, picked up the tab on life but she didn't want a stranger telling her. She turned to the safety of 'the husband' and started talking about this person who did not exist but would know exactly how to sort this lot out.

Belle wasn't having any of that and said Ramon had screwed up his drawing and thrown it into the pool.

It made Mia laugh but she kept it short. She was too hurt and angry.

'The group is down to a couple of people,' said Belle. 'The little guy with the goodwill, Cynthia, me, the other over-fleshed girl maybe. Eric would join us but the well-dressed hag pays his bills.'

'I would rather stay here,' said Cynthia. 'And have a rest and some treatments. And the private art classes with Mia. Really happy to pay for that. They are priceless. And Mia, I'll cover your meals.'

Mia was too angry to speak but Belle said she thought what they had agreed about running a group was a good idea. 'We can use the experience to work on ourselves.' She looked at Mia. 'There is no point withdrawing. Don't let them win. You are a light-bearing person.'

Mia was ready to reply savagely but remembered her bank balance. She could, she realized, manage the days at the spa with Cynthia's input and probably more from Dick Topper. 'I'm not upset,' she lied. 'I'm used to working with movie stars. This lot! You don't have to get the Kleenex box out for them.'

'Did you really work with Shelley Winters?' asked Belle.

'She's fabulous,' said Cynthia.

'Not painting. It was supposed to be. It ended up me sitting with her while she directed scenes at the actors' studio.'

'New York?' Belle asked.

'LA.'

'She lived on Melrose. I went to her place,' said Belle. 'Powerful lady.'

'What did she want you to do?' Cynthia asked.

'Tell her if I thought she'd gone too far. I seem to have lost that skill.'

'And?'

'She'd already started too far.'

'Are you stuck for money?' Belle asked.

'Of course not,' said Mia closing down now.

Cynthia coughed meaningfully but Mia did not choose to change her story. Cynthia spoke for her. 'I think we all have moments where we do our best and expect the best back. And that's what's happened here.'

Belle looked at Mia's proud reaction to that idea and knew then she was definitely broke.

'Are you here for the group? You must be disappointed,' said Belle.

'Of course not,' said Mia. 'I've been here a long time ago. And I thought I should do some paintings here and....' Her confession stopped without the mention of Sal Roca.

'Sounds good to me,' said Cynthia pouring more tea. 'They've got fish pie for dinner. Thank God we don't need to be on that silly diet.'

'Let's agree a sum we need to run the course and get the little guy in too. I think Maggie might donate. And Lily is stuck because of her return ticket which is non-flexible.'

Mia stood up. 'I am not dealing with them again.'

'OK. If you change your mind....' Belle looked at Cynthia. 'You could do it.'

Her reply was instant. 'I don't know anything about it.'

'You just follow the itinerary,' said Mia.

'Do exactly as it's written,' said Belle. 'By the way, Mia, you haven't lost face. Just tell them the whole thing, especially that the asking for

90

money was a workshop from LA. I can vouch for that. And it brings self-knowledge. It makes us sharp. They'll be begging you to do it, offering you the whole trip and fares to Sedonia or wherever the "in" place is now. And Maggie is au fait with LA and knows a few smart people so get a bit more up to date with who's there and what they're doing. I see her waiting for you to trip up.'

'I did work there but it was over eight years ago.'

'Hollywood is a cruel town.'

Mia asked what she did.

'I'm a hostess. I look after people.'

Mia and Cynthia were immediately interested.

'A hostess as in the old days? In nightclubs?' said Cynthia. How she hoped she was.

'I have a set of people who come to stay and I make sure they have a good time and meet the right people. And my husband of course. I look after him. Travel with him. It's all high end.'

The two women sat absorbing every word.

'But right now, we have to decide about the coach.' Belle liked running the show. 'In other words, are that lot still on it? And after a short time in Girona do we, as the itinerary states, go north to the mountains?'

'Can you pay for it? The coach?' said Cynthia matter of fact.

Mia looked up at Belle. She was definitely the right one to ask. She wore the accoutrements, from the canary diamond rings to the rubies in the ears, of The Saviour.

Belle shrugged elegantly and the diamond neck chain tinkled. 'I think we're here to kick start our lives. To find solutions. Not take the experience of doing that away from another person.'

'So, it's no,' said Cynthia. 'Let's try Dick Topper. Someone said he's a magician.'

'I will start resolving this by sharing this room with you so cutting the cost into three.'

Was she mad? thought Cynthia. The jewellery said she was not.

'We need something to restart us and get our clocks ticking. A challenge,' said Belle.

'I think we've got enough of those,' said Mia.

'Jump out of a plane, hope the parachute opens,' said Cynthia.

Belle was thoughtful. 'Running over mountains.'

Mia was taken aback. 'Do you mean actual mountains?'

'I used to. I still could. We all should.'

The others were silent, totally unconvinced.

'We are like those men who get stuck in a mid-life crisis. You know the story. And they go and get a new woman and that's not the answer. They suddenly want youth.' Belle nearly choked on that. Of course, the bastard would get some extreme nubile sylph.

'And?' said Cynthia.

'Some race cars or learn to fly or cross deserts. But the best is to climb a mountain. Kilimanjaro is always the favourite. The men come back reborn.'

'But these climbing people are in their forties,' said Cynthia. 'I don't need to remind you we are not.'

'It works. It's a rite of passage. We've all seen 40 but we can do it. So, let's run along a mountain. . . .' She added, 'range.'

That was never going to happen.

Little did they know it would happen.

Belle's mobile phone rang and took her by surprise. She ran out of the room and down the stairs speaking loudly. Cynthia opened the door. 'Sounds like Russian.'

'Nordic.'

'What is it about her? Why would she want to sleep in here with us? Doesn't make sense,' said Cynthia.

'There was the little matter of the credit card.'

'I just can't call her Belle,' decided Cynthia.

'Why not?'

Cynthia squeezed some limes and added cold sparkling mineral water. 'And all that hostess-pleasing-men thing. Do you think she's a hooker?' Cynthia looked at her seriously.

'I do hope so.'

Chapter 13

Maggie and Belle had one thing in common although they did not know it. There was something about Mia that disturbed them. For Belle it was nothing obvious. She preferred Cynthia who, whatever happened, was secure in her unashamed appetites. The young husband amused Belle. The considerable land and small properties were reassuring. Even Cynthia's exuberance of flesh, too extreme now to be hidden, was comforting. Her largeness in life soothed Belle. And then she understood why Mia irritated her. She didn't have a spread of life but just a pinch. She was a loser. Belle would rather give her money than do her classes. Then she remembered she didn't have money.

Maggie saw from the start that this individual, Mia, was a loser. She hated losers. And then uncomfortably she understood why. Wasn't she herself a loser?

In Belle's case the irritation diminished and she started to enjoy the qualities Mia did have. The tired old repeats of exercises for the Hollywood has-beens became a way out of the acid anxiety greeting her every morning before she'd even woken up.

Belle's son said he was appalled by the news she had left her home in the company of Van Gogh. 'You can't keep it.'

She explained Jasper had always had a thing about youth and she had kept it going. Until… She could hardly blame her son's age and baby and asked how the baby was doing.

'Yes, I heard a bit about that young girl thing he has. Do you want me to mediate?'

'Please don't!'

'Can I help in any way?'

She asked where he was and he said Washington. Then he said, 'Did you love him?'

What a strange question. 'No. His power was the turn on.'

'I don't really know you....' He nearly said, 'Mum.'

'I've done my best,' she said. 'You got it better than if I'd stayed in Oslo West.'

'Let me know if I can do anything. But make sure if you by any chance did take the picture you give it back.' He hung up.

'What a little shit!' She sat on the back stairs and thought of all the schools, universities, good opportunities, great jobs, she had given this little shit. It took her mind off the increasing pain like a wound inside her.

Mia was in the spa kitchen arranging with Carlos a sugar-low, protein-high dinner for Cynthia, Belle and her. She also asked about the general state of things in Catalonia. She was even going to say the name of her one-time lover, Sal Roca, but heard the group arriving in the spa bar. She hurried towards the dining-room exit but Maggie was in full sight at the counter. Two back steps and she was behind a white screen which blocked off a lavatory.

'He's got a lot to say for himself that Englishman,' said Maggie and poured Ramon a drink.

'I was actually going to hit him,' Ramon realized. 'But then he'd have probably hit Eric.'

Eric laughed. 'I'm so glad you didn't.' He touched his face, his beauty still intact.

They sat at a table only yards from the screen and Mia.

Esmee joined them.

'Say what you like,' said Maggie. 'It's not our fault. To suddenly have it sprung on you she wants a hundred a day! Just who is she? '

'Well it worked,' said Eric. 'I felt a new way of approaching transformation. Instead of going from sitting position using thought to get us through, she gave us primary shapes. I liked it. My painting as I absorbed it into my thinking became a vortex.'

'Like a portal?' said Esmee.

'A vortex sucking me down.'

'What good is that?' said Fatima, exasperated. Only her return ticket to Dubai kept her safe.

Eric had years of experience in meditation, spiritual rituals and

94

sitting practices. He'd sat with all the best teachers in India. He was entitled to call himself a stage 1 initiate. 'I like what Mia did.' He explained why and the atmosphere became almost positive until Maggie said, 'I've never heard of her. I'm going to look her up. What's her full name? She soon stopped asking for money when she realized, we're not an easy touch.'

'I agree,' said Esmee. 'People come to these sorts of groups without a coin to their name and say Buddha, or whatever, expects we all share our goods and benefits because it makes us better people. Sai Baba used that one. Condition of entry to ashram ... drop your entire material goods right into his lap and if you were seriously well-off you got a blessing and could be front of the daily queue for his healing. But we have to look after Lily. All this trying to adapt to these usurpers is making her ill.'

'Lily is here, Esmee,' said Eric quietly. 'At the bar.'

'You forget one thing,' said Ramon. 'Kelly Brooke let us down.'

Mia, still stuck behind the screen, did not know how to get out. Her legs were starting to tremble from the standing and the stress. She would back off into the lavatory if one of them moved but she needed to hear or couldn't not hear the rest of their opinions.

'That's not the point,' said Maggie. 'These women, and they work like a team, have taken over and want money for it.'

'At least it's something to do,' said Ramon.

'By the way, have you paid?' asked Maggie.

'My room and board. I'll see how it goes.'

Mia looked at the girls sweeping the floors. I'd rather scrub them on all fours than teach those bastards.

Cynthia decided if Mia could get through the art class fiasco, she in turn must do something in support. But what? 'I used to teach.' That was all in the past. She realized she just had her day-to-day life to draw on. 'It can't be a demonstration of old English cooking?' For a moment she might have found the answer.

'No, it can't,' said Belle decisively.

How crestfallen Mia looked, too silent in the corner, with the once hopeful brushes and unused palettes just strewn around her. 'If you can do it so can I. Flower arrangement. They'll get it and like it. And pay,' continued Cynthia.

'Try sightseeing,' advised Belle. Get a guide book and show them the village. It's only one street. It can't go wrong.'

Cynthia wasn't sure. 'Sightseeing? A group? They'll end up lost in some bar. Or I will.'

'You don't have to do it for me,' said Mia. But Cynthia was already hurrying to the garden, feet swollen, legs aching.

Eric said the group was delighted if Cynthia could do a session. Sightseeing was one thing but what they really liked was Cynthia's classy voice. 'I think what it really comes down to is they would love a chance to speak like you.' Was this a joke?

They were all outside the origins of Cynthia's upbringing so there would be no criticism and bad behaviour there. Would they like to practise some patterns of speech? Vowel sounds? They would. And they would pay for it. Lily, Fatima, Eric, Ramon and Esmee started towards the gate. Even Dick Topper said he'd give it a go. Eric called up to Maggie in her room. 'What about it?'

'Don't be ridiculous. You'll come back with some green belt approximation of upper class.'

Cynthia decided to focus on English appreciation of rural life compared with the Spanish and, carrying a handful of guide books, led them towards the church. Nothing could go wrong with this.

Wrong, Cynthia? Remember your attention span. You can talk about anything in any accent for almost three minutes but it all comes down to Ed and you take usually one listener as hostage to hear the illusory joys of life of Ed and everything else is forgotten. A dangerous loss of attention in this case.

It was only after the final oiling of their bodies that Mia and Belle realized the sun was low and Cynthia absent. 'They'll be having a good time. Probably in some bar,' said Belle.

Mia wasn't so sure. After the clock chimed the hour, she suggested going to look for them. Belle said it was only a small village so what could happen? Hardly had the last word been spoken than Cynthia dragged her away, one shoe missing, through the gate. They hurried to rescue her and, breathless and sweating, she was placed in a chair.

'I've lost one.'

They thought she meant the shoe. 'If only.... We can't find her anywhere.'

Belle knelt beside her. 'Tell me who!'

'Lily.'

'Thank God not Fatima. Then we'd be in trouble. With her background she wouldn't be lost but kidnapped.'

Eric and Dick Topper had split the group to search in the few bars and fewer shops. Her mobile was not on.

Cynthia admitted she had started off with a look at village life encapsulated in green belt accents, emphasizing the vowel formation, and then the image of Ed at the golf club came to mind, filled her thoughts and she found herself talking exclusively to 'nice Esmee Pont' and as usual when that subject started then everything else ended. Cynthia didn't think she'd spoken for more than a few minutes — it was over 20 — and the others after waiting had gone variously into shops or the church. Cynthia remembered pulling herself out of the reverie of the married life she should have had and restarted the talk on diction. Eric gathered the others back but no one noticed Lily wasn't there.

'Cynthia wouldn't notice if she was there,' said Belle.

'Please don't say this to Maggie,' said Eric, 'She'll live off it for a week.'

Ramon took the car and sped towards the woods. Yes, there was a local rumour about a no-go area for women.

'It's too awful,' said Cynthia in her perfect pronunciation. 'First The Cat. Now Lily.'

Maggie turned to Mia. 'What shall we do?' She didn't know. 'Well, you're the one who should. You're the leader.'

Cynthia took Mia's arm. 'I'm really sorry. I didn't notice she'd gone.'

Any more than you'd noticed she was there. This mirage, known as Ed, has lost you so much and now it's lost a real person.

'It's not our responsibility if she's just gone off,' said Cynthia. No one had the heart to say, 'Not ours, yours.'

When Lily allowed herself to be found and brought back, she said

Cynthia had been busy talking to Esmee so she had said she would wait for them in a shoe shop but the women took no notice. 'When I came out you had all gone and I started walking and the anger went and the feeling of being left out went and I started to notice the countryside and I felt free....'

'I'm so sorry,' said Cynthia. 'I must never take a group. My speech is one thing. My counting quite another.'

Maggie turned to Eric. 'At least she said that with almost no trace of green belt.'

Maggie appeared at dinner admirably dressed and in a softer mood. Eric, very attentive, was quick to pull back her chair at the head of the table.

'I've been thinking about this trip. Beggars can't be choosers and maybe the meditative painting interweave is good for us. Also, she knew this area years ago, and although no spring chicken has got her facilities.'

'What is that to do with it?' said Ramon.

'She remembers how things were. She's also good on the atmospheres and patterning of landscape and maybe can be helpful for locating the Grail Cup. It's somewhere in the vicinity. We've been assured of that by the right people.' She looked at Eric and he nodded.

'The map lays it out clearly. As it once was. We can find it ourselves. We don't need her to follow the map,' said Esmee.

'Really?' said Ramon. 'I can remember it gave that cop a laugh.'

'We simply attune to the atmospheres,' said Eric.

'We can pendulum the map,' said Esmee.

'I'm sure we've all done that,' said Maggie.

'Did The Cat know the whereabouts of the Grail Cup?' asked Eric thoughtfully.

No one answered. They all looked at Maggie. It seemed since The Cat's outrageous absence each one took over as tour leader. From Lily it passed briefly to Mia then onto Maggie and she was hanging on. Eventually Eric said Kelly knew about it obviously.

'I looked up her early work.' Maggie was talking about Mia. 'It was promising. I like some of it. The atmosphere again. Edward Hopper, *Journey to the End of the Night*. I know that's Céline but you know what I mean.'

Esmee said she did.

'So, what are you suggesting we give her?' said Ramon.

Maggie shrugged. 'Her early work was really something. First exhibition at 21. She got the reviews. I even spoke to Bea and she said Mia Zang sold to actors like Dennis Hopper. That's how she got into the teaching. She's the real thing. Was. Offer her half.'

'Fifty a day!' said Ramon.

'It's above my budget,' said Esmee.

'Oh, do stop it,' Maggie was exasperated.

Lily was silent.

The three women were not in the dining room. They were being served dinner at the usurper table beside the pool, the night air exquisite.

'Where's the Englishman? He's not with them.' Maggie peered through the rising steam from the hot pool. 'If he's a magician he wasn't exactly magical bringing up the art class fee just as we were starting to paint.'

'Dopes like that always cause trouble without even trying,' said Ramon.

'It's his fault,' said Maggie. 'He should have been discreet. If he's a magician let him use a little magic putting this back together. Maybe he's checked out. Go and ask at reception, Eric.'

At the usurper table the women planned the 'conquering of the mountain'. Belle explained the process of preparation. Workout, then sharp workout, relax, out of the body travel....'

Cynthia asked if she'd done that.

'Not knowingly,' said Belle. 'I can always try. We use the running. We can run in our minds and here on the ground reaching another paradigm.'

'How long will it take?' said Cynthia.

'Let's just go towards it.'

'I like it,' said Mia.

'What sharp workout? I don't like the sound of that,' said Cynthia.

'No, you won't at first. You run as fast as you can full out for two minutes. That's it.'

Belle planned an early start taking the breakfast session at seven and off across country stopping for brief exercises on the way.

'What, tomorrow you mean?' Cynthia was appalled.

'I do mean tomorrow,' said Belle.

For the first time Mia felt happy. It was so far beyond anything she could envision doing.

And then Cynthia asked about Dick Topper. Where was he? What if he came to their table? Mia said he had probably left after all that happened. At that moment he came striding through the main gate. He approached their table smiling and said he had gone for a long walk into the countryside. Polite conversation followed and then Mia said he should join the real table inside the dining room.

The three women sat in the card room playing Blackjack. The group sat in a reception area playing Bridge. Cynthia had had a cursory conversation with the enemy, mentioning strong protection as the sun was deceptive. Maggie cleared her throat and looked at Eric. 'Notice that choice of word. Deceptive. I always distrust overweight people.'

'Careful,' said Eric. 'There's one at our table.'

'Two,' said Maggie.

Cynthia was mentioning some products to Fatima. 'Upkeep of salt and liquids.' No problem with liquids at that table.

Cynthia carried two ice-cold glass mineral water bottles to the card room and said she felt calm, even optimistic. The card room was old fashioned and reminded her of the 'parlour' of her youth. 'You don't have them anymore.' She tried to describe the tiny comforting room with fireplace and books, present in most middle-class homes. 'Mostly used for women.'

And then the chief cop from the Girona night chose to enter by the garden door.

'Thank God he's in plain clothes,' whispered Cynthia.

With a nod and a smile to those over in the reception he came straight across to the parlour card table. Belle immediately looked down; her cheeks unfortunately flushed.

'You play one game and they another. Is it just a matter of card games?' he asked.

'Are you a mind reader?' said Mia and invited him to join them. He pulled up a chair and Cynthia asked his name. When it came to it Cynthia had the authority. She had the social graces.

'Gerard.' He peeked at Mia's hand then at Cynthia's. He pointed to the card she was about to lay. 'I would choose. . . .' And he pointed at the Ace. 'That one. What do you think?' He looked across at Belle as she was busy trying to arrange her cards. 'Can I call you Belle?'

'Of course, it's my name.'

'Does an Ace take a Queen? Or does the King?' His voice was soft as Cynthia said later, 'It stirs you up.' She hadn't had that feeling for a while.

'Maybe it's a matter of how many coins accompany the King,' Belle said sharply. 'Then we can decide who takes what.'

He was amused. 'Of course.'

Belle laid the Queen.

'Well played,' said Gerard. 'So, the Queen takes the King and the coins.' He waited for her to look at him. Her eyes lifted by mistake and linked into his. No escape and all thoughts of walking over mountains were quite gone. His expression was strong and demanded a response. She gave it. It was obvious what she felt. He'd got what he wanted and half laughed.

Mia offered him a drink and he called the waiter and asked for a Cortado and Cognac.

'Why are you here?' said Belle and her voice shook. Only deep breathing would get her through this. 'Is yours an official visit?'

Again, their eyes met and locked in a so-necessary and private gaze. He leaned across, poured her some water and held the glass to her lips.

Cynthia examined her nails. 'I'm going into the treatment rooms tomorrow,' she sounded matter of fact.

Belle took hold of her glass and put it on the table shakily.

'Have you any word of Kelly Brooke?' he asked. And at last was able to release his gaze and look at the other group. 'Has she contacted you?' He turned to Mia. 'I hear you run the group.'

'I did.'

'So, it's not just a matter of a different card game. This being in two groups.' He laughed again; his laughter always short. He didn't often get atmospheres wrong.

'We don't know anything about her,' said Cynthia. She had to concede Gerard was very attractive. A mixture of power and sexuality. It was obvious he fancied Belle.

In the other room Maggie laid down her cards. 'The cop is the answer,' she said softly. 'Maybe Topper did work a little magic.' Smile already in place she got up and walked absolutely straight and sober into the parlour. Gerard stood up acknowledged her arrival and Maggie asked if he and the others would like to join her and the group.

'Maybe we should all join together for this matter.' She smiled warmly at Mia. 'I would appreciate your help.'

In the other room Ramon warned Eric to play it down. 'The cop is a little senior for this sort of thing. He's not just a local guy on the beat.'

'Think this takes a cup of strong coffee all round,' and Eric called the waiter.

Cynthia made the decision, nodded at Belle then asked Mia to help her up. 'I ache from all the exercise.' Gerard took her other arm and they arrived in the more formal room. For some reason they all sat in a line against the wall.

It made Mia laugh. 'It's like we're in an ID line up.'

'Where's the Englishman, Richard Topper?' said Gerard.

'Is this an official question?' asked Ramon.

'Just a little concentrated effort to try and help find your friend the teacher.' He stood at the abandoned card table and checked his mobile phone and then looked swiftly at the different hands abandoned on the cloth. He pointed to what would have been Eric's lucky finale. 'Nice hand,' he told Eric, remembering he had sat there.

'You obviously play,' said Eric.

'Only Poker.'

Eric tried to sound light. 'We must have a game one evening.'

Maggie hissed a warning. 'Drink anymore and we'll end up arrested.'

There was no answer from Dick Topper's room and Maggie said he was probably asleep. She asked Gerard if he really needed him. 'What do I call you, by the way?'

'Gerard.'

'For now,' said Eric and laughed.

No one joined that laughter. In different ways they all felt uneasy.

Cynthia spoke first. 'I've just remembered the other name for parlour. Nook.'

Eric tried not to laugh. 'I think Cynthia's tired.'

'Exhausted,' she promised him.

Eric suggested she go to bed. After all she had never met The Cat.

'Only her absence,' she said sharply.

Ramon chose to speak and cut through any more tipsy time wasting. 'Officer, I have to be clear on this. I am a consultant oncologist in. . . .'

'I know where you work,' said Gerard.

'I came here simply so my partner could experience Ms Brooke's amazing work. . . .'

'Yes, we've spoken to him,' said Gerard matter of fact. 'Please stay because something might occur that's helpful.'

Lily held her face as though to stop her mouth saying inappropriate things. Mia felt awkward that she had seen The Cat only as a nuisance and hadn't cared about what had happened to her. She had thought only of herself.

It took only a few minutes to establish that no one had seen her this time. Three people had read her books, four had been to previous courses. She had never behaved like this before. They did not know where she lived but she did frequent a bar near the hotel in Girona and sometimes took a room there for private sessions. Gerard turned a page in a small notebook.

'Did she have a mother here? Or grandmother?'

Mia looked at Lily who in turn looked away.

'And you?' Gerard turned to Mia. 'Perhaps you think someone present knows more?'

The large reception clock ticked loudly. It was five minutes past midnight. They were supposed to start their 'mountain' programme at seven. Suddenly angry she turned to Lily. 'You should say what you know so tell the truth and spare us all this.'

Lily didn't answer. 'And what's that?' said Gerard.

At the risk of making Lily an enemy for life Mia said, 'She's been in contact. And I'm not just referring to the first night when you, Lily, were supposedly on the phone to her and she was five minutes away.'

Cynthia sighed. 'Just find her. She's caused enough trouble.'

Belle turned towards Gerard. 'Is all this why you're really here?'

He turned to look at her. 'No. I'm here for you.' He closed the notebook.

Belle wanted to say, how can you come into my life like this?

Maggie said the interview was concluded and stood up. 'Has anyone seen her, Gerard?'

'When I have something to tell you, I or one of my men will do so.' A second thought made him say, 'Can you give me a copy of the map?'

Eric had one folded in his pocket. He straightened it out on the table. 'It's just a kind of game,' said Eric.

'That's what I thought,' said Cynthia pleased.

'Is it?' Gerard gave it back to Eric. 'It's old. Who made the copies?'

'Kelly Brooke,' said Eric.

'With whom did the maps originate?'

'A little trouble with your English there,' Ramon laughed. 'She must have got it from an archive. Eighteenth century.'

'Seventeenth century.' Gerard corrected him, said goodnight, left money for his brandy, touched Belle, his hand lingering on her shoulder. 'Stay out of the heat, Astrid,' and left.

Suddenly Mia ran after him. 'Gerard, stay and see something of what we do. We are about to do a short healing on Ohm.'

He hesitated and quickly she got the others into a circle outside by the big pool. 'One of us stands in the middle for some moments and receives the healing sound Ohm from the others in the circle. Then that person changes place with another who then stays in the middle. It's important to keep chanting Ohm without pause so we keep the force going. It is healing.'

104

'I certainly need that,' Gerard said and went to the centre of the group.

Why had she done this? Mia thought it was to keep him there for Belle. Whatever, it certainly healed the group.

Eric said afterwards, 'We look forward to another art and meditation class tomorrow. When do you want to start?' And he handed her an envelope of money.

Chapter 14

It was everything Belle and Gerard thought it would be. It was inevitable. They got every moment, every delay, every high, before the climax. Hungry, immediate, desperate, the act of two people starved for the right kind of love. They hadn't even left the spa garden. Afterwards he held her gently, not speaking.

She thought, if we speak, we spoil it. I had better speak. I cannot feel like this. Not *this* good. It can't last. 'I didn't expect this,' she said.

He laughed dryly. 'Oh, you did. From the first moment.'

'Are you going to take me in?'

'No,' he said.

'You make a lot of big decisions for a cop.'

'I'm not a cop, Astrid. I'm an intelligence officer.'

'Yes, my husband would only go for that. High up the ladder?'

'I make decisions.'

'Why aren't you looking for the Van Gogh?'

'You're not a thief. You aren't that kind of player. You've had a rough deal.'

'But how did you find me?'

'It takes two minutes.'

She was surprised.

'I'm C.I., Central Intelligence. The hotel register. Your passport.'

'Do you know what it's about?'

'I think he's a tricky player.'

She told him some of the truth.

Gerard laughed. 'Now you're playing the other way. You are never 50. You are having me on.'

'Can you keep me safe?'

He pulled her on top of him. She hadn't had it like that for years. Afterwards he took her to the sea and showed her the places he loved.

'Do you . . .'

He put his hand on her lips. 'No questions.'

'How do we...?'

'We write our script. Some women can't go without a man for long and Belle is one of those. Or Belle is restless. She's never been without a man. Belle can't get enough.' And he took her again by the side of the car. Afterwards he said, 'That nearly took me somewhere else.'

They sat in the car outside the spa and she said she would leave for Girona. 'After that I don't know.'

'Forget the coach,' he said. 'I can get you a private one. How many people?'

'Ten if they're still on.'

'They're on,' he said.

'Why?'

'They want to find the Grail Cup.'

'Do you?'

He put his arms around her and really held her. 'I think I've found it.'

'Are you...'

'No questions, Astrid. You know better than that. Give me the documents tomorrow and I'll get them copied and take them to your husband, rather common-law husband.'

She looked at him. Could he do that? He could do that. She would never let anyone do that.

Cynthia, still awake, asked Mia if she was asleep. The words crawled across the silent room like a shy insect uncertain of arrival even if one existed. Mia had not slept at all and lay on top of the bed very still. She had been denied all sleep. Her body would not relent from its almost dangerous rigidity brought on by jealousy. Rock hard holding tight. Was this how the Grail Cup or object was supposed to feel? She also knew Cynthia had been imprisoned by a terrible insomnia because not one snore had escaped all night.

Cynthia decided Mia was too still. 'Awake?' said Cynthia still softly but needing to talk.

'Definitely.'

'I heard five strike. She's not back. I would have heard the key.'

'She's with him.'

'Of course,' said Cynthia. She sat up and through the shutters saw the light changing. 'How old is she?'

'I think when you're that well taken care of it doesn't matter.'

'He's married.'

'Definitely. I bet he's a good lover.' She drank from the water bottle. At least she could now move.

'Do you remember all that?' said Cynthia.

'Yes, and I miss it.' She tried to persuade herself she liked the feeling of freedom, of not needing the highs and lows. 'I remember. How can I forget? That electric elation. That deep soul connection.'

'Oh don't. You've obviously had it.'

'The first was the one I remember now. What about you?'

'Only in books.'

'Husband?'

'Let's not start on him or I'll never sleep. He is not my husband. I'm tired of lying. It's exhausting. I had a husband. That's how I got the title. But I left him for Eddie Coy, my common law husband.'

Was this good news?

'It's rotten. We argued for three nights so I came here exhausted. I can't live without him. '

'Is there anything I can do?' She knew there wasn't.

'He's 22 years younger than me. He's where life is.'

'I wouldn't do anything right now. How long have you been with him?'

'18 years. He's good with my children.'

'What do you really do?'

'Look after the kiddos. Seven grandchildren. My three children are from my first husband. His lordship is probably well pleased by this disaster. He's on his uppers apparently. Ed has money. He's in finance. Lucky. He's at the right place at the right moment when the action happens. He's a trader. Hedge fund. My son says he's a launderer.'

'Do your children dislike him?'

'Ed doesn't let you dislike him.'

Mia thought this was one for Belle. She'd have the ideas. She advised Cynthia to get in good shape. Use this time. She couldn't but see the exuberance of flesh through the nightdress that clever garments had carefully disguised.

Cynthia said it was a commonplace story where she came from. 'In the country it's not mentioned. The women get on with their gardens and the village fêtes. It's all community. That sort of thing. The husbands are in the city. They come back at weekends. Of course, some of them have a mistress or two in town but it doesn't matter as long as they play the game when they're home. It's the look of the thing. Isn't it?'

Mia didn't know.

'At least we didn't let her share our room,' said Cynthia relieved. 'Imagine if she had had him in here. All that going on.' She laughed, a wonderful, full, releasing laughter.

'Do you want a cup of tea?' said Mia.

'Might as well. It's after five.'

'At her age,' said Mia laughing again.

They were both so jealous they decided to exclude her and forego the wonderful experience of 'claiming the mountain'.

They must have slept because Belle was moving around the room and the sun was fully up. Splashing and shrieks of joy from the pool.

'We've missed the first breakfast,' said Cynthia.

'But not the second.' Belle gave them each a cup of coffee. 'Amazing day.'

As long as she doesn't talk about it, thought Mia, I can manage. She put ice on her eyes to discourage the bags and wrinkles. 'It's a shame. I was so looking forward to starting the preparation for the mountain. Cross-country running, wasn't it?'

'But we are doing it,' said Belle. 'Let's do some exercise first.'

'Are you invincible?' and Mia realised Belle showed no signs of a sleepless night.

'I've had it easy. Now although it's a little harder I'm not too bad.'

'Maybe if the cop has as much stamina as you, he can take us to the mountain,' said Cynthia. 'He looks fit.'

Mia almost laughed.

'We don't need to pay for a coach back to Girona. He'll provide it.'

'Is that your going-home present?' said Cynthia.

Mia laughed, then stopped. Maybe Cynthia wasn't joking.

'I'll see you at breakfast,' and Belle was gone leaving a slight trail of delightful perfume.

'That was a bit off of me,' Cynthia admitted. 'But she looks too good.' Cynthia managed to get to her feet.

'But you've got a young husband.' She shut up and drank the coffee.

'When is this coach supposed to come? Is it today?'

Mia could not remember.

'I'm not going. I need to stay here. Another day,' said Cynthia.

'Sure,' said Mia. 'We can decide what we do.' Then she remembered the envelope of money and the agreement to do an art class. She let Cynthia have a shower first and simply splashed her face, cleaned her teeth and noticed her knee was discoloured. Somehow it didn't look like a bruise. We get fragile as we get older, she told herself and took care as she went down to breakfast.

Cynthia said she could not do cross-country, remotely and couldn't even get to the spa gate. She was going to have a rest and some massage treatments. She was quite firm about it and to show she was her own person she ate traditional buns coated with sugar, two fried eggs and tomatoes followed by pain au chocolate. She saw Dick Topper looking across with admiration and smiled, the first smile of her day. Not looking at either Belle or Mia she said she was not taking any coach that day.

'We had better tell them,' said Mia. 'But they have paid for the tour.'

Belle was shocked. 'What? How much?'

She pulled out the envelope and Belle counted the money. '530. Well, I can guess who gave the 30. The mean French artiste and she's got a whole block of apartments above Nice and still owns a club in Paris. You're lucky, because this only buys five of them and the 30 is a tip.'

'I'll postpone the coach till tomorrow. I'll go and tell them. I'll postpone the Girona hotel and ask if we can keep rooms here.'

110

'Do the last thing first,' said Belle. 'Then I think you and I should start the practice. You only have to take four fast steps, then take it up to six.'

'What if this group doesn't want the deal?'

'Give them the class. After lunch. And they can go to Girona in a six-seater cab this evening.'

Eric was OK with a change of plan and said he would handle it. Maybe they could all go running with Belle. She doubted it. 'We could paint some rocks,' he suggested. Mia liked that idea. He looked at the discolouration on her knee and said it was only the skin. 'Maybe Esmee can give you some healing. She is a powerful healer. Lily could certainly handle some too. We've got a new girl arriving in Girona so I'll have her make her way here. She's been with us once before. From Chicago.' Then he looked at her face. 'Get rest, not more exertion.'

'Of course, you can run this group,' Belle told Mia. She was still in her original room combing out a second wig. Blonde with plaits. Mia said she liked it better than the dark one. The truth was whatever Belle wore she couldn't lose her beauty.

'I use them in carnivals and parties. The pink or pale mauve are the best. They might give cop a turn.'

'He likes you,' said Mia.

Belle didn't even react. Her mobile rang again and she clicked it off. Mia knew the caller was Gerard.

'Let's go and walk fast. We'll run later. Bring a bottle of water.'

While Mia climbed the hill, which gave a view of Mount Canigou, Cynthia lay covered in mud in a hot wrap having her feet massaged.

'Do you want pressure point?' the therapist asked.

'The lot,' said Cynthia.

'Just get her in touch with stones,' said Maggie. 'Or a rock.'

Eric knew the place. A small sacred circle of stones used by the Romans, a short walk from the spa.

'We carry the painting equipment there and get her to do psychometry first. She's a sensitive. She'll get a connection. Then show her the map and let her use the pendulum. The title of the workshop is "Finding the Grail Cup".'

Eric was not at all sure.

'Tell her just like that. Then we paint and draw. For all I know that's why she is here. For the Grail cup. She didn't come for the group. Never heard of Kelly.'

'Do you actually believe it, Maggie? The Grail? Here?'

'Kelly Brooke did.'

Belle wrote the menu in French for Carlos. 'The group has to stay off sugar. Zero sugar.' She looked at Mia. 'And she has to have carbs but the others don't. Carlos, we can have that wonderful spaghetti with cheese, olives, fresh tomatoes, herbs.'

'And fresh greens.' Carlos was getting excited. 'Baked apple with cinnamon and I can do a sorbet, unsweetened, with real fruit.'

'Of course, you can,' said Belle. 'But here's what you can't do but you will do. Nobody drinks.'

Carlos shuddered. 'And what if...?' The thought made Carlos pale under his tan.

'They just eat elsewhere, no longer part of the group. We are here for transformation.'

Belle's phone rang again and she went outside. She told Gerard she had to have time to think about the papers.

'So, you're staying at the spa,' he asked. 'You'll be safe there.'

Astrid, you're not safe anywhere. Careful with the Cop. Keep a big distance there. Papers? You're not giving him even a paper tissue.

The trouble was she fancied him like mad. She ached for him. That bad! She sat on the ground suddenly. Mia had been waiting for her and asked if she was alright. Belle didn't answer. And then Mia understood.

'I'd go for it if I was you. Life is so goddamn short.'

'Are we talking about the cop? He's a one-off. He's married. I'll start to need him. Disaster. It's all downhill.' She nearly said, 'And I'm getting old. The upkeep is terrible.'

'You look after yourself, Belle.'

'At a cost. I don't have the luxury of being like you.'

'Oh, all that is years ago, the art...'

'I meant your spontaneity. I have to think twice.'

Belle went into the quarrelsome lunch. 'It's all downhill from last night, all downhill, down, down.' Over and over like a mantra.

To get her mind off Gerard she talked about the past. Belle admitted she was 53 and still absolutely in love with a Frenchman 20 years younger. She decided she had to trust her two companions and showed them a photograph of a shaded hotel room. She stood by the window, as though looking out but her body, dressed only in a silk slip, was turning towards the bed where the Frenchman was lying watching. He seemed to be smiling. Or was it the way he frowned to avoid the sudden spear of sunlight? Belle, her face in shadow, could be any age, her body slight and well-toned was apparently youthful. The Frenchman wearing pale shorts was well made and as the French say 'good in his skin'. He was as Mia said later 'on top of his game'.

'No, we never made it,' Belle said before the women could even ask. Yet everything in the photo said they had.

'It's better than anything I've seen lately,' said Cynthia thoughtfully.

'It's the atmosphere,' said Mia. 'A shot from a film.' She couldn't let go of the photo. 'It's private and has drama, a French movie.'

'From the '60s,' said Cynthia.

'Or earlier. *The Lovers.* Jean-Moreau. Or *A Man and a Woman.*'

Cynthia asked when it was taken.

'Last month,' said Belle and finally reclaimed the photograph.

Mia blinked. 'You mean this last month?'

Belle slid across another photo showing her and the Frenchman walking through the gardens of the world-famous Eden Roc Hotel, South of France. How similar their walk. Their feet tilted at exactly the same angle. It was as though they were going to break into a dance. His right foot, her left, both lifted as though to take the first step. Their sweaters although a different style were of the same blue. His jeans, her scarf, the blue was repeated as though they were wearing the coded uniform of their love. This much they could allow to be seen.

'You belong together,' said Cynthia.

They walked separately, not touching. He slightly in front had turned to look at her amused by something she was saying.

'He's class,' said Mia. 'Charisma? No shortage there. It's clear he likes you.'

'Definitely.' Cynthia was enthusiastic.

'You can feel the attraction. It's there in the photograph.' Mia did also notice one difference. Belle looked old. 'I would do anything for what you have. Even for an hour.'

Defiantly Belle took back the photo. 'Why do you talk about it in the present tense? It's long past.' And the evidence of the love affair was taken back and buried deep in her bag. 'Don't read too much into it.'

'So why show us the photos?' said Mia.

'Because...' Belle did pause. 'I thought something might happen. I just wanted you to know. About that one afternoon.'

'Happen?' said Mia. 'To you?'

'I might...'

The women waited. Belle finished the sentence, '...die.'

Cynthia decided not to speak.

'Something about this place,' said Belle. 'It's dangerous.'

When Mia and Cynthia were alone, which they seemed to be increasingly, they agreed on one thing. Belle and the Frenchman had been lovers.

'That's quite a hotel,' said Mia. 'I've been there in the old days. I think it's the Eden Roc. She paid for it.'

'No,' said Cynthia. 'He has money.'

They realized they could talk openly. They felt comfortable together.

'But why did she show us the photos?'

'In case something happens to her so we tell him.'

'But we don't know who he is or anything about him.'

Later when Cynthia asked Belle why she hadn't slept with him Belle said, 'I was too old.'

Mia lay on the bed seeing clearly in her mind the photos of Belle and the Frenchman in the hotel room and walking in the grounds of the splendid hotel. Two people with plenty between them. Secret, private. It was only when she was almost asleep, she asked aloud, 'But who took the photograph?'

Chapter 15

Cynthia, pummelled, oiled, soothed and stretched, felt the best she had for months. She took the lift from the treatment area to her room although such an ascent was banned by Belle who took stairs even when she didn't have to. Sometimes Belle would run several flights every hour. Cynthia, grateful for the calm and emptiness of the room, fell back on her bed and decided two things. This would be for now her way of life, and before the second, which had something to do with her husband, she fell asleep.

Belle pushed Mia the last yards and got her up to the top of the hill. From here they had a magnificent view of the countryside and Belle pointed to the sacred mountain, Canigou. 'There it is and we will claim it.'

Mia, out of breath, was naturally about to lie down but Belle insisted she stretch and jog on the spot. They got back just in time for lunch.

'Why do you keep making me talk as I walk?' said Mia.

'To make sure you can breathe.' Belle slapped her shoulder. 'You've been in good shape at one time. It's served you well.'

Mia felt good in herself and felt she had taken a real step forward in fitness and stamina. Ramon got up from his table, followed her to the stairs and took her arm. 'Have you had a blood test lately?'

'I'll do it when I get back.'

'I'll do it for you,' he said gently. 'For a doctor I'm not bad with those needles. Even my partner lets me take his blood.'

'I will. I just have to get this over.' She didn't say what the 'this' was.

'How long have you been losing weight?'

She'd noticed it that morning having breakfast in Girona. The haggard look.

He said if she needed anything to let him know.

116

Back at the table Maggie said how well Mia looked and the discolouration on her leg had almost gone. 'She walks almost as good as me.'

Ramon sounded serious as he said, 'It's not that. It's the loss of weight.'

Eric rushed his second pudding to get over to the Romanyà Dolmens to take his daily photographs. Art class was sharp at five and Maggie wanted him to get some pieces of ancient stone. He felt sad and thought it was to do with Ramon's warning words about Mia.

Cynthia was woken from a deep sleep and answered the mobile automatically. A grandchild asked if she was home. When was she coming home?

'Why, darling?' said Cynthia and just for a second she wasn't sure which of the nine (or was it seven?) grandchildren she was talking to. The toxic dream still claimed her thoughts.

'It's Joey's birthday tomorrow.'

Was that Joey the child? Or her eldest son's dog? 'Oh no!' And it all fell into place. She told a young Becky she'd sort it all out and ring back later.

She got to her feet and splashed her face with cold water as Mia arrived triumphant in the room. 'I actually started running. And Cynthia you look great.'

'They've oiled my hair.' The mobile rang again and Becky's mother asked what flight Cynthia would take.

'Ed will pick you up. Do you want us to get the cake?'

'Oh shit...,' said Cynthia and the connection was cut.

'Say you're ill,' said Mia immediately. 'A non-dangerous virulent bug you certainly don't want to give to them.'

Cynthia sat on the side of the bed biting her lip, a habit Ed detested. 'I don't know what to do for the moment.'

Mia made the tea. 'I think this place is what you need right now. I've just swum ten lengths. That's a first.'

'I haven't even sent a card. It's funny but this is the room where we make decisions.'

'Certainly is. I've got to do the art class at five.'

'I've not missed lunch?' She sounded more alarmed by that than anything else.

'They've put aside a salad for you and I added a chocolate eclair.'

After Mia's shower Cynthia decided the virulent bug was the answer and she would take Joey out for a whole day in London when she got back. 'They always have the tea at my place.'

'Let Ed do it!' And Mia laughed.

Cynthia didn't laugh. 'They knew I was going for ten days. What else have I forgotten?' She sped through her diary. 'Is Belle seeing the cop?'

'I think she was trying to tell us it was a one-off. That's why she shared those photos. I just wonder who took them.'

A second cup of tea got Cynthia 'straight' as she called it. Something in the back of her mind needed attention but she couldn't reach it.

Belle, wearing the blonde wig and shorts which deserved their name, carried in Cynthia's lunch on a tray. The eclair was missing. Mia winked and indicated it was secreted in her bag. Cynthia, sitting with her increasing fat around her emotions, had another choice to face. She'd keep the tempting eclair for later. Belle had marvellous legs, strong, lithe, lightly tanned, flawless. 'You must have been a model.'

'Only for my husband.'

'I should have done more of that perhaps. I don't know what I'm doing here.'

'How did the trip come about?' Belle sat down. 'Do you usually take trips alone?'

'Never.' Cynthia described her ever expanding family.

'So how did you, the matriarch, take this trip?'

Cynthia explained how it came from Jenny a new girl who worked for her husband. Jenny felt Cynthia needed a break more than she did and gave her the booking.

Belle, onto Jenny immediately, helped Cynthia to see this trip was the prelude to yet another of Ed's infidelities. Obviously, it was Ed who paid for it so he could get Cynthia out of the way and be free to sleep with the girl. 'How old is she?'

'Young. New. She runs one of his health clubs.' Cynthia wanted not to believe it. She believed it. A call to her house was all it needed. The cleaner said Ed was down at the pub.

'Alone?' Cynthia added, 'I hope not. Don't want him to be lonely.'

'No. He's with that young one who runs the health gym.'

'Jenny,' said Cynthia.

'Jenny,' the cleaner agreed.

'So, let Ed put the spread on Joey's sandwiches,' said Mia.

'I should go back.'

'Put yourself first.' Belle and Mia almost spoke at the same time.

Yes, this was what the dream had unleashed. She had felt guilty at being away but who had sent her away? 'He must be serious about this one. He doesn't go to such trouble to secure the others.'

'Spend a lot of money,' said Belle. 'His money. We'll go and have a special fish lunch by the sea. And let's go to the spa shop and get you some creams.'

The Decision Chamber, as it got to be called, did cheer Cynthia. After ravaging the predominantly green leaf salad like a demented rabbit, she went to her next underwater pain-relieving sulphur bath almost happy. Later she realized she was relieved. It had surfaced. She no longer had to live a lie.

Eric arranged pieces of rock trying to follow Maggie's instructions. 'Mia has to hold them so not too big,' she said. 'And she must pendulum them. Let's see what she gets. I am sure she is clairvoyant. And must be in the area for a purpose. No doubt the same as everyone else's.' The venue had been changed to the spa garden.

Belle counted the money which she asked for in advance. 'Another 30. That's from Green Bow again.'

'Let's do psycho-drama,' said Esmee still wearing the green bow.

'Absolutely not,' said Belle and added softly, 'At 30 euros. We will do psychometry. The trees, the rocks...'

'I think we get more out of confronting ourselves,' said Esmee.

'Confront! We've done enough of that,' said Belle.

Ramon lay out the chairs.

'I'll talk to you about the rock,' said Eric to the group. And he told them again about the Grail Cup and they all liked that. That it could exist. 'And we know it's here. We are privileged. We have these rocks that come from the same timescale as the Grail and can be a vibrational pathway.'

Maggie gestured he include Mia.

'So, let our guide show us how to use our own intuition when picking up an object,' he said. 'Let's see if we can sense the elusive hiding place.'

'Great!' said Mia doing justice by her quick enthusiasm to her many years in America. 'Psychometry. Why not?'

First, they used 'the holding of the stones', then the pendulums appeared and Maggie asked questions about the power of the stones. Next came the Grail map and they all had a turn to pendulum its power.

'What do you get?' Maggie asked Mia.

'Nothing.'

'Why not?'

She shrugged.

'That's hard to believe,' said Maggie. 'You're a seer.' She turned to Eric. 'She's blocking.'

Belle beckoned to Mia to stop the pendulum swinging. 'They are using you. Change the subject.' Belle suggested painting.

Esmee was disappointed.

'I thought we were doing psycho-drama.'

You'll get just that! Psycho-drama! Not long now, Petite Chanteuse.

Mia put a chair in the middle of the group. 'Sit here, Lily. Tell your story. And then the group heal you with Ohm chanting.'

'Sounds innocent,' said Maggie.

It began innocently enough. Lily stood up. 'I'm hating all this. It's nothing personal.'

'Of course, it is,' said Maggie. 'It's always personal.'

'It's so amateur. It's not Kelly. It's a waste of energy.'

'You're 54,' said Maggie. 'You're going through a menopausal afternoon.' She turned to the group, 'She's looking for Mr. Right.'

'The only 54 is Studio 54,' said Belle. 'That was a night out that lasted three weeks.'

'Don't give your age away. You know all about sleepless nights,' said Maggie.

'I don't have sleepless nights. I have nights out,' Belle corrected her.

Maggie turned back to Lily crouching now in her chair. 'Worn out, looking after her aunt, menopausal, hormones not doing it. Always been on her own. Lightning would have more chance of striking the same place twice than her finding a Mr. Right.' Maggie sounded calm.

Mia told her to shut up.

'Shut up?! That's a bit out of character for the Little Match Girl on the edge of debt. Daren't say Boo...'

'Are you talking to me or Lily?'

Lily cut in. 'It's me.'

Maggie replied, 'Actually it's her. Mia.'

Eric thought he was changing the subject by suggesting painting would have been a better idea after all. He turned to Maggie. 'You won't get anyone showing what they can do holding stones if you go on like that.'

'Match Girl, Boo to A Goose. Makes you ill. Say your truth. You daren't, do you?' Maggie taunted.

Trying to keep cool Mia said it was all from the past, all this resentment and anger.

'I like winners,' said Maggie. 'Not Match Girls. They get a bad deal and go one hundred percent behind getting it.'

'Who in your past made you a Match Girl?' Mia stared at Maggie. She had stolen all the good of the day. 'Bets on your father.'

'Don't speak to Maggie like that,' said Eric.

Belle turned on him. 'Stop saving everyone.'

'Why don't you try? Start with yourself!' said Lily rough.' Screwing cops doesn't quite do it.'

Belle stayed on Eric. 'So, what are you?'

'Just a sharer in your scene.'

'You should be so lucky.'

121

'You just walk on across the ice, over the coals and you think what worked 20 years ago will still cut it for you. Don't you see and feel your truth?'

'Don't cross-examine me!' she spat.

Mia was deeply uncomfortable. Esmee was hiding under a chair either frightened or emphasizing this was psycho-drama. Mia wondered if she should step in and conduct the dialogue as though it was psycho-drama. She asked if anyone else would like to play this scene. 'Let's stop and take a look at what we've got.'

Eric turned to her. 'The stones have brought out a lot of suppressed feeling.'

Belle jumped on him. 'Don't keep protecting her. What, is she your grandmother?'

'I think we stop it here,' said Cynthia suddenly part of the ring. Her hair was covered in thick white soap. 'I had to come and see what's going on. Let's just do some balloon breathing which I do with my grandchildren.'

'Oh, do stop!' said Belle. 'This is not a perfect world, Cynthia. Live in the real one.'

The exchange became worse and ended with Dick Topper throwing a chair.

'We will need a real magician to put this right,' said Maggie.

Esmee stood on the chair clapping with excitement. 'It's the best!'

Belle turned on her. 'Don't live off other people's lives. You live enough off their rents.'

'Oh, oh. Below the belt!' said Maggie.

'You started it,' said Lily.

'At least this little skirmish in the heat did something. It made you speak up,' said Maggie.

Mia told them all to lie down, and cool down. 'Let your body go till the ground supports you.'

'It's your fault,' Maggie told Eric. 'You started it.'

'Me? I never said a word.'

'Exactly!'

To relax took a long time. 'Mia should have simply divined the

122

rock with the pendulum. Much simpler.' Maggie thought she'd sorted it all out.

'I told you not to eat shellfish in the heat,' said Eric.

Afterwards Lily was put back on her chair and she was game for a try at 'storytelling'.

'What is its purpose?' said Ramon.

'Forget purpose,' said Mia.

She had realized one thing. Maggie was a much better facilitator than her. She had the courage, the elegance, the education, the class. She was sure of herself.

Sometimes she can't get through the next five minutes. Ask her.

So, Mia asked Maggie how she was doing. How is your life?

'I find it hard sometimes to get through the next five minutes.'

Chapter 16

'How did Belle know?' said Cynthia. 'That Ed is not exactly faithful?'

'You have referred to it a couple of times obliquely,' Mia answered promptly.

'Obliquely! Belle doesn't miss a trick, does she? What about her husband? Has she any children? She's certainly not a grandmother.'

'Now I think about it, it's hard to pin her down.'

'She is slippery.'

So far Mia had only seen her as kind.

The moment was fast coming when Belle was not slippery enough.

The weekly spa dance by the pool with live music, rumbas, paso-dobles, waltz, rock. Cynthia would never miss that. The coach was put off another day.

Mia remembered those dances in the Sal Roca years. Nothing had been as thrilling as those local dances and maybe nothing ever was.

'I'm just going to wear casual clothes,' said Cynthia. 'It's only the spa clients. Eric will be in great demand. Do you think Belle will come?'

As Mia put on her new creams, a conciliatory present from Maggie, she thought, why wouldn't she? That was suddenly an important question. She was going to mention it to Cynthia but the dance music came sweetly up through the garden into the room. 'There seems to be a lot of voices.' It didn't make sense. And then she heard a voice that could not be there. Ash Phoenix singing one of his hit songs.

'It's a recording with audience background. For a moment I thought....'

'Did you know him?' said Cynthia.

'My second husband did when Ash was just starting out. And now he's one of the best ever....'

The voice of Ash Phoenix was hypnotic. He was known for that.

Ready for a nice casual evening they bypassed the lift and took the stairs. Out into the garden, surprisingly quite full, no one was dancing but standing and watching. The crowd from the arrival evening in Girona including Lou and Josie by the pool, and there in a white suit, quite simple, stood one of the music greats, just singing for the love of it.

Belle ran down the back stairs and danced her way towards the band in full view of every eye — this a slippery moment indeed — and a hand grabbed her arm and stopped her. 'Back off,' she said and turned to find Gerard already pulling her behind a bush. 'Get to the car. Stay in the trees.' He turned to make sure no one had spotted her. The singer in the white suit had turned around and looked puzzled. The artist with the tattoos next to him turned too. Gerard waited but they carried on with their evening.

She sat in the shadow in the back seat. She asked what he was doing here.

'My job.' He laughed. 'The unpaid one. Looking after you. That was a close call.'

And then she heard the voice again. 'That's Ash!'

'Yes, I thought he'd know you.'

'What the hell is he doing here? No one comes here, for Christ sake.'

'He's got a concert in Barcelona and is staying on the coast with...' He read from his phone. '...movie people from the US. And Kelly Brooke's group has gone there too. They decided to come up here to dance because they like authentic places. Bal Musette. That sort of thing. The wig and glasses don't quite do it. You need a mask.'

'A Venetian carnival mask,' she said. 'I've got quite a few of those. Maybe one in the luggage. Thank you,' she said softly.

He kissed her and started the engine.

'How did you know Ash would come here?'

'Reports come in from security. Quite easy. He has his own guys but they let us know where they're going.'

'He's been at my house in France. Maybe twice. I don't know him really.' She was shaking again. 'I think I've got it together and a way forward, and then something else comes up...'

125

'Jasper Jay's lawyers came up. So, let's just give him back the documents and deal letters you took. And you sign their deal letter that you stay quiet.'

'Why should I?'

'You may want to go back.'

'I'll never go back there.' The way she said it, she meant it.

'Where are the papers?'

'I've got a son and he recently had a daughter.'

Gerard laughed. 'So, you're a grandmother. You missed that out last time. It's just a number. That's all age is. A number.'

'So, I'll keep the stuff. Rainy day. Flight fund. Magic money.'

He turned the car round and told her to keep low until they were through the gates.

'Get the stuff and I'll do the deal.'

'Why?'

'He's very rich and therefore powerful.'

The crowd from the coast couldn't believe how great Cynthia was looking and then the singer approached Mia. He had a lovely smile. 'Hi, Ash.' She held out her hand. He ignored that and hugged her. 'I often wondered how you were doing. I was really cut up when your old man died. He had such a range.' He took her across to a table away from the group.

'Did you recognize me?' she asked.

'Your bones. Your smile. But they told me you were here. Lou and Jo. We've been friends for a while. And I met Lily. She came by to Sean's place. I've been clean for a few years. I had my problems. I know you tried to get him off the stuff.'

'Addicts are amazing,' she said. 'He blamed Hollywood and said the dealers wouldn't leave him alone. So, we moved out of Holly-wood to a gentle place full of peace. But then a stray dealer drove by and someone pointed at our house and said a rock-star lives there. We were miles from the main action. The dealer comes in. Then a whole lot of dealers come in. So, he said let's move to a strip of coast south. Nothing on it. Just sea and a lighthouse. So, he put me and the kids in the place and set up his music room. No one will find us here.

126

So, what does he do? Jumps in the car and drives back to the city to the drug dealers.'

Ash said, 'It's called doing a geographical.'

Then a girl wearing a carnival mask came through the trees and danced till dawn. Only Mia knew who she was. And the C.I. cop sitting at the bar.

'I don't know whether to break with Ed.' The three women were sitting in the Decision Chamber. Belle told Cynthia she was the only one to decide that.

'I can't bear the thought of going to dinner alone,' said Cynthia. 'I mean the social things. And people having to find a partner for me at dinner or bridge. It sounds so pathetic.'

'It is not pathetic,' said Belle. 'It's your reality. It is not pathetic.'

'And they'll say he left for a younger woman. This age thing is a nightmare.'

'Telling me,' said Belle. 'Don't divorce him. Spend his money.'

'It's actually my money he's spending.' But it had originated from ancestors Cynthia didn't exactly admire. At least the means they used to get the money.

'Money is neutral,' said Belle.

Cynthia had gained weight dramatically and the clothes could no longer hold it in. Her bosom had settled on top of it all like two plump cushions. Her makeup made the most of things but couldn't hide the life exhaustion. Mia thought this image didn't belong to her. She was not who she should be, battered and betrayed. She should act on stage. The voice. People would never tire of that.

When Cynthia went to wash her hair, Mia said she's comfort-eating and the fat comes on fast.

'It's the drink,' said Belle. 'She drinks with both hands.' She looked out at the overcast morning. 'I actually prayed she will get the right man. '

Cynthia lay on the bed without drying her hair. 'You are carrying all this guilt. Let alone all the weight. Let's go out and do a workshop on Cynthia's divorce.' Belle dried the brave yellow hair with a towel and massaged her neck.

'Oh God, I don't want them to know.'

'They've got enough hiding their own stuff. I meant a small workshop, just us,' said Belle.

Cynthia couldn't get up. 'I feel this room is my reality. It won't happen again. Too old.'

'Let's go and do the class,' said Mia.

'Do we have to?' Cynthia was horrified. 'What about the coach?'

'Gerard can fix that.'

'I don't want to go today,' said Cynthia. 'I really think I need a rest. You go if you want.'

'I like it here,' said Mia. 'But the Grail stuff is in Girona.'

'Really?' said Belle.

In Mia's case the Grail was Sal Roca.

'We can call the tune,' said Cynthia. 'Let's put it off one day.'

Every day by noon the coach was cancelled and rebooked for the following day. The truth was none of them wanted to leave this, which Maggie termed 'Oasis of Discovery'. She had originally chosen 'peace' but that had to be rejected after psycho-drama session number three.

After the third treatment-packed day, and apparently, sugar and carbs-free diet, Cynthia seemed better and the exhaustion had gone but her weight had not. It had not only not reduced; it had gone up. She put one toe in the world of exercise and started walking with Belle and Mia as far as the hill but not up it. Water exercises in the pool were for a kinder day. The weight increase puzzled Belle and Carlos. What was different about her life? The answer came from Maggie. 'When our friend Cynthia says she'll forego supper for something she calls fasting it coincides with someone else also not taking supper.' It took Belle and Mia too long to work out who. 'Dick Topper,' she said.

'Well, that's coincidence,' said Mia not allowing rumours about her friend to grow in the steamy atmosphere of the spa bar where Maggie presided and made all social decisions. You were in or definitely out!

'He's hired a car,' said Maggie.

'Wish he could've done that a bit earlier,' said Belle.

'By the way, what happened to your car? Lamborghini wasn't it?' said Maggie.

'Too small to be any use.' Gerard had had it secreted in a garage; numbers changed.

Maggie waited. Did these women have to be quite so slow? 'She's been seen out with him.'

During the following pause Mia felt almost offended that she had to hear gossip about her friend's activities from this woman.

'Maybe they are looking for the Grail?' said Maggie laughing. 'Well Mia doesn't seem to want to find it. You know you can channel what's out there.'

Mia had already realized Cynthia seemed happier. Maggie turned to Belle. 'You want to put Gerard onto them. Or maybe more earthly matters make her look better?'

'How do you know?' said Belle always preferring to receive information than giving it.

'Twice they've been seen having dinner at first-rate places in the countryside. That's where all the best restaurants are, incidentally. And a lunch at the Three Star Roca brothers' place in Girona. You normally wait a month to get a table there. So, ask yourself...'

'Ask what?' Belle was snappy.

'If they're having an affair. It's their business,' Maggie offered her an opening.

'Exactly,' cut in Mia. 'Let's get their opinion on the food and book a group visit.' She walked away with Belle rather than running upstairs to confront Cynthia.

'Odd choice,' said Belle.

'What do we do?' said Mia.

'Do? Nothing. I would have said she goes for alpha male types, or she did in those days. Maybe your preferences change as you get older.' Mia doubted it. And then Belle remembered her prayer for Cynthia to be well accompanied. God did it His way. Or had a sense of humour. They agreed to keep quiet so Cynthia could have some fun.

'One thing, it can't go wrong,' said Belle. 'No one else is going to take him.'

As soon as Belle turned towards the pool Mia couldn't wait to rush up the stairs. She was going to handle it delicately. Just a little friendly exchange between grandmothers. Seeing Cynthia sitting at the mirror surrounded by newly purchased creams, her hair red-gold as the sunset, Mia was sure.

'I can understand you need to get even with Ed but . . .' What came after the 'but'? 'If you had talked to me, I would have said Dick Topper is not the one for that.'

Cynthia looked at her as though she'd lost her senses.

'Are you having an affair with Dick Topper?' She could see it was childish. Was Cynthia suddenly her mother? Her daughter? Cynthia either blushed or the new cream was the wrong colour.

'We like the same thing,' said Cynthia.

'Please don't go into details. It's your business.'

'It's very naughty really.'

'I don't need to know all that!'

'Oh gosh! You don't think that do you? "They" don't think I'm having a thing with him? We both like food.'

'I've noticed.'

'We both like it a lot. And I can't bear this one salad leaf thing. And he loves good food. So, we creep out to other places. I didn't think we were spotted.' She put on more eye makeup. 'I didn't want you or Belle to think I wasn't trying and appreciative.'

'Apart from the appetite what's he like?'

'He knows how to choose good wine. He sees cooking and pre-paring food as alchemy. Belle got me all wrong. Dick saw that immediately. I would have told you. I did think of asking you and Belle but all that denial of sugar and pastry is too much. We just enjoy food!' Mia lay down, her aching leg on a pillow.

'Where are you going next?'

Cynthia turned; her eyes full of mischief.

'He likes to give me a surprise. So, I can't tell you.'

'So, do you think you'll be back in time for the art class and psycho-drama?'

'Oh, I'm here for lunch. I'll be out tonight.'

'So, you won't be sitting in on the poker game?'

'Oh, don't make me choose. By the way, in normal times do you like chocolates dark? With mint cream? He's bought me such a selection. Really super stuff.'

Carlos who soon heard of Cynthia's unimaginable betrayal placed a plate of pasta stuffed with cheese, aubergine, olives, fresh tomatoes, capers and green herbs in front of her, followed by an undoubtedly teasing glance. Eric who had also been told of the monumental dis-loyalty to 'slim', introduced her to the new group member from Chicago who was some days late as she had stopped off with the famous ones on the coast. The girl was petite with hair that stayed perfect in all conditions and was a pinpoint perfectionist. It was hell for Cynthia because she just wanted to turn loose on the pasta and enjoy the decent glass of red wine Carlos said went with it. He added, 'You might as well have it. I'm now making your dessert to match.' And now she had to make conversation with a girl who did not reciprocate. 'Yes' and 'No' did it for Cherie. Eric turned and couldn't miss the interaction. He raised his eyebrows playfully. He knew what he was doing.

Cynthia managed to get a menu for Cherie although it was after lunch hours. The girl took her time reading through the dishes and Cynthia's good heart went out to the stranger. Her remaining pasta now cooling, she translated as best she could the starters and main course. She then gave a little advice on what to choose.

'Do you like rabbit?' The pasta was now past its best and Carlos whisked away the oversized plate.

When the girl didn't answer Cynthia suggested the fish and to start, the gazpacho.

The girl put down the menu. 'If you don't mind, I do understand Spanish. I know what I want.'

Cynthia said later she had had fun wondering what that could be.

'Lobster.'

'Lobster, as in a whole lobster fresh or...?'

'Yes of course.' Cherie put her glasses on and really looked at Cynthia.

'I haven't actually come face to face with a lobster here,' Cynthia admitted, 'But they have excellent grilled prawns.'

'I eat lobster. Kelly Brooke knows that.'

'So, Cherry...'

'Cherie.' The girl corrected the mistake instantly.

'You want lobster and just lobster at every meal?'

'That's right.'

Cynthia managed to get Carlos' attention and explained the requirement.

'Impossible!' He didn't waste time.

'Can we provide them for ... was it Cherry? or Cherie? ... for this evening?'

He said, helpfully, 'Her name's Sherry,' and took off his apron. 'Kitchen's closed.' He was gone.

'How long are you here for, Sherry?'

'I'm doing the group. Same as everyone else. My name is Cherie. Can you arrange for a bucket of live lobsters to be delivered every day and very cold?'

Cynthia then got what she thought was happening. This was psycho-drama punishment for her creeping off into gourmet heaven and tempting another diet-client to sin as well.

'Kelly Brooke always fixed this for me. I eat three a day. I have paid for them.'

'Anything with them?' Cynthia added. Like the word 'please'.

'Just fresh lobster. When do we start? The art meditation.' She looked at her very expensive watch. 'I'd like to start now. I'm never late.'

And Cynthia began to get the idea this was not psycho-drama, simply drama.

Carlos brought the mocking dessert filled with meringue, clotted cream, scoop of colourful ice creams covered in 'hundreds and thousands', confetti and across the top in glistening chocolate, 'Welcome Back'. Hardly had she put the spoon to her mouth than a bombardment of flashes blinded her as everyone including the staff seized the chance of immortalizing—Cynthia thought it sounded like, 'The Glutton of the Summer'.

Cynthia deprived of a wonderful lunch arrived late as the group was starting meditation. Cherie still wearing her classic Chanel jacket, sat too upright in a chair. Nothing got through to her that she didn't invite, thought Cynthia. Then she saw Eric half hiding behind a tree trunk. She beckoned for him to join her. Obedient he led her swiftly towards the building. 'I know you think we did it on purpose for a cheap laugh,' he said.

'I do,' she said. 'But Sherry wants lobster.'

'Yes. Well she would. She did before too. Or maybe then it was crayfish. Easier to get.'

'This is paying me back?' She tried to laugh.

'No, not at all. Shereen just needed a motherly figure to look after her a bit. You know how it is.'

'I don't.'

'Cynthia, people *like* you because you're warm and accessible.'

The compliment sounded almost as good as the dessert had tasted. 'What's wrong with her?'

'She's just like that. Works for the government. The wrong government of course. She's a whizz on IT. Seriously world class.'

'What's wrong with bringing in Lily?'

'She's depressed. It doesn't look good. If you can just do a bit of that grandmother thing, Shereen will warm up.'

At that moment there was an altercation as the thin, unsuitably clothed newcomer wanted to disrupt the meditation and have her place moved into the sun.

Chapter 17

Belle helped Carlos choose herbs from the countryside. She picked berries and edible flowers. 'I love the smell of thyme.' She was in her element in the true nature, a child of nature. 'I so miss picking the berries,' she said.

He asked where she came from and she described her Norwegian summerhouse on an island at the end of a fjord.

'You must come here and pick the mushrooms in season,' he said.

She told him on this short walk she felt unashamedly happy. 'It's when you get to people ... another story! I pray for peace.'

Her mobile rang as they arrived back at the spa gate.

God didn't hear that prayer! And she stayed still to receive the call.

Her son sounded short and almost hostile. 'Here's what you have to do.' How American he sounded. 'Listen, Astrid, and don't think you can make this a better deal. Your lawyer will meet you today.'

'Where?' She was right not to trust Gerard.

'And you will give your lawyer everything you took from the house.'

'So, my former partner has been onto you?'

'He's been here. You've taken ridiculously heavy stuff. You can't use it.'

'What's my end?'

'He leaves you alone.'

'What about you?'

'Me? Why do I suddenly matter?'

'I've done it for you ...'

'I don't really know you, Astrid. There's a lot of things about you that I don't know. I just know I have to look after myself. He's heavy, he does not take hostages.'

'He's just another little boy inside an old persona.'

'It sucks, Astrid. And you can't go to the press with this.'

'How's the baby?'

'That subject is way off this conversation. Off limits.'

'So, I don't get to see the baby?'

'No!'

His 'no.' How like hers.

'He's got to you because he knows I care about you,' she said. 'That's where I'm vulnerable. So, I don't have a choice. I can have the stuff dropped at the lawyers.'

'Thank you, Astrid.' He disconnected the call.

It took her a long time to get over that call. She stood by the wall of the spa half hidden by trees until eventually she got upstairs to her original room. Cynthia was fast in comparison.

'I should have been a better mother. Correction. A mother.' She spoke as she wrote with an ink pen. 'I did want the life Jasper Jay offered me and I went for it. The deal was no children. Not negotiable. I saw the son Jasper had no idea about when I could, but mostly he was at school. But I did love that little boy but I could not let myself get too involved. I couldn't bear the missing him. I had to be a winner. That's why the young bit had to happen. J.J. only liked girls. No one aged slower than me. I got away with it because he was hardly there. I was just an acquisition keeping his legend going. The hostess. I wanted to be free and I thought that life gave me that. Now I can be free. Whatever that is. Love you.'

And she addressed the envelope to the man in the photographs and sent it by the local 7 p.m. post.

She heard the other two go back to the Decision Chamber but felt too down to join them. It wasn't that she would end it. Just that an epoch of a life had ended. She didn't need her lawyer to tell her J.J. would not negotiate. He would not negotiate. Not one buck. Gerard who was not without intuition told her he was a 'dangerous, mad tyrant' who would want to punish her, not because she lied about her age, but because he could not control ageing. He needed to control life. And what a disappointment he got. Gerard arranged to meet the lawyer in Perpignan just over the border in France that evening.

'No discussion,' she said.

'There is no discussion,' he promised.

She lay on the narrow spa bed with its correct mattress and wrote several letters to her son. They were all in her mind. The best thing she could do for him was to leave him alone. And the little girl. As she went to sleep, she thought of her true home. The home of her childhood. The summerhouse on the fjord. That was where she was really herself.

'You don't need a wig anymore, Astrid.' It was Gerard speaking. He was in the room. She could smell the black tobacco. 'You can drive your Lamborghini. I brought it here for you.'

She sat up, drank water, looked at her phone. Looked at him. 'Thank you.'

He sat on the bed. 'If you want your things . . .'

'I don't.'

'. . . from the house.'

'No.'

'He's put them in storage.' He gave her the key. 'You think you don't want to know about him but you will want to know. You're safe. He feels he's dumped enough punishment for one lifetime. Personally, I don't think he'll sleep well at nights. Where do you want to eat?'

She laughed. 'Somewhere cheap.'

'Where am I going to get a pail of lobsters?' said Cynthia. She'd woken up with all the stress and worry of green belt-style life with Ed. It made her see she'd been living with the impossible. 'I got too much sun.'

'Take a pill,' and Belle looked on the night table. She was dressed ready for the morning exercise.

'Oh, I never take pills. I only take natural things.'

'That's crazy. It's not a natural world. Take a pill. In this life you have to accept a certain amount of compromise.'

Cynthia sat up. Ed was impossible because what he wanted, she could never give him. She realized she was his mother. She was everyone's mother. It was easier to get a pail of live lobsters in the middle of burning hot countryside than please him.

136

'Let Carlos deal with it,' said Belle. 'They have frozen fish delivered daily.'

'She wants fresh not frozen. Where is the fish market?'

'It's Carlos' job.'

'He won't touch it. I had her, Shereen, crying all night. Then the spa owner Señor Torra had to join us. He said simply, "Carlos, my chef, is upset. So, I have to choose between you and my chef. And I'm not going to lose my chef." And he made Shereen a hotel-booking up the road. She's quite fragile and I feel sorry for her.'

'So why is Shereen still here?'

'I said I'd look after her. She's been through a lot. Never had enough love.'

'No one does,' said Belle.

'It can't get worse,' said Cynthia.

It could. Eva with the skull was waiting downstairs and wanted to speak to Cynthia. She carried the skull wrapped in a blanket like a baby.

'Why are you here?' asked Cynthia. 'I thought you'd abandoned us for those A-list ones on the coast.'

Eva peeked at the object in the blanket. 'It says this is the place to be. Do you want to see it?' She started to open the blanket.

Cynthia certainly did not. Eva herself was a surprise. She had imagined this person who had booked a room with two beds in Girona and not left it for a moment, would be some pale lifeless hermit. This black, vibrant, bright-eyed life-loving sprite who travelled the earth on wonderful adventures had to be the star of any group.

'I need to talk to you. That's what the skull indicates.'

'This minute?' said Cynthia.

'I feel I'm being reached by the Grail vibration. I get no sleep.'

'Will you come with me to locate some lobsters? And then we can sit down and have a cup of tea.' Cynthia's head ached and she knew it was the second bottle of 'wine beyond price', the previous night. It didn't matter whether it was pure grape, chemical-free, 'cost the earth' or 'cheap supermarket' running with additives, it was still alcohol and if you drank enough the hangover was the same without mercy.

137

They needed more space for the meditation after the Ohm healing, breathing the balloon and, with eyes closed, body still, the listening to sounds faraway, medium distance, close to and internal. Mia asked for each one in turn to say why they were here.

'What is this group about?' Shereen cut in strident. Her voice itself, a machine, all emotion and colour driven away long ago.

'This group is about someone who isn't here,' said Mia.

Maggie showed surprise.

'It has been all along.'

'Interesting,' said Maggie.

'So, I want you all to describe The Cat. One at a time. Whether you know her or not.' Mia chose Lily to start.

'I'd rather say why I'm here,' said Esmee. And she started saying why she had left the main group and returned to this group. Mia didn't care, as it happened, who said what as long as it wasn't her. The weather was heavy, a storm predicted. She felt 'out of sorts' and could just about sit up, her back against a tree. Before long she knew the session would progress to her lying flat in a star position. Belle had counted the money and said Mia was now in pure profit and then unusually had gone off on her own.

'I was on the coast but I like it better with you,' said Esmee. 'They may be the new stars but they know nothing. Haven't even heard of Johnny Halliday or Yves Montand. All they do is go on those machines which kill your brain cells.'

Shereen as Cherry, Cherie, Sherry disliked the reference to machines and said so.

'You or just Napa Valley, kill the world. Why should this beautiful planet be destroyed so a few people can be rich?' said Esmee.

'I love that,' said Eva. 'The skull is happy.'

'The money is too big to dismantle,' said Shereen.

Eric looked at Mia waiting for her to show a facilitator's touch here. 'Maybe the absent one is actually present with the A-list lot at the coast,' said Mia. 'It occurred to me a few times.'

Eric laughed. 'Can't get the point here. We are all here to look for and find the Grail Cup. Something tells me that it's not on the sea-shore.'

'Why not?' said Mia.

'Because since the Grail Cup landed on this planet the sea levels and tides have changed considerably. Something so valuable would be placed in permanent safety. That's what the old map tells us.'

'Such as...', said Mia feeling they were getting somewhere now.

'High,' he said. 'Mountain high. And protected from the elements, floods, wild animals, bandits, fires.'

'So, a cave,' said Esmee.

'Not bad,' he agreed. 'Except it has to be dry. Or the moulds would coagulate.'

'A cave,' Mia felt cold.

'I think we go back to the reason why we are here,' said Maggie just in time. A man with a large leather expensive rucksack slung on his shoulders, had arrived soft-footed at the edge of the group.

'You've got my room!' He looked at Belle.

She asked him to join the group or go and wait by the pool. He was agitated on the edge of angry, needed to rest, had been travelling all night and had booked the room which should be vacant today but she had stayed on. The spa had nothing else.

Mia looked at Cynthia whose eyes closed, shutting it all out, the weather, the hangover, the people, life. Eric wasn't moving. He told the man to go back to reception.

'There's no point. I've just come from there.'

'I'll go.' And Cynthia got to her feet thinking it can't get worse. It could. Shereen followed her saying she was very hungry, wanting the lobsters, and Eva and the skull, wanting her attention got up too.

'That's Jonas Boon,' said Maggie. She waited for the reaction. Nothing in that circle. Mia told them to lie down in the star position and let the ground hold the responsibility of their bodies. 'Just let it go.'

Mia went straight to the fountain and drank the spa water and considered how to get out of the afternoon 'changing thoughts' session. Cynthia was coming towards her through the heat and seemed years older than when they first met.

'What is it about today?' Cynthia said.

139

'In your case, last night.'

'You're right.' She asked if the spa water was alright to drink. 'Are people like this, usually? Have I been sheltered? The lobster eater will not give in and Eric had to drive to a supermarket to get frozen lobster. She's got all the emails agreeing to this dietary requirement. I think I want to strangle The Cat. Maybe someone already has. No one's seen her. I can't bring myself to look at the skull. And the man called Jonas Boon is well known for being a nightmare on metaphysical courses. What is this nightmare?' Cynthia splashed her face and the sulphur water dried instantly in the burning sun.

'It's called being a tour leader.'

Cynthia laughed. 'Why don't we just chuck it in and go and see the local psychic? Supposed to be good.'

Belle walked across country towards the sacred mountain. It was a spontaneous activity that she hadn't planned and she didn't even carry a water bottle. She felt she was in the catchment area for disaster and would get ahead of it if she kept on doing what she always did. Fly. She ran through the heat and sprang into the air, dog-paddling her way upwards, defying gravity. And for a few seconds she did. She walked onto the next village, the only person out in that heat, turned the corner to the bar and Gerard waited in the shadow. He was carrying a glass of her favourite drink and she swallowed it in one go.

'You girls from the place of the long dark days sure love the sun.' He felt her head. 'Let's get some lunch.'

'Did you follow me?' she said.

'In this heat? The watchtower picked up your trail.' He pointed to the furthest hill.

The lunch was long and cool and final. She thanked him for all he'd done for her. He said he wouldn't forget her. At least for a week. 'So, you want to disappear?'

She thought she did. 'I've realized since being here how someone who does disappear draws all the attention and focus. "She was like this. She never did that. She seemed alright." Or, "If only I'd known her."'

140

'Are you talking about Kelly Brooke?'

'Of course. It's all about her this trip. It's crazy.'

'So, you're paying him back that way.'

She shrugged.

'The lawyer called me with a deal,' she laughed. 'But he's cobbled it together from an asset here, a pension there. Not anything anyone would notice. Not even J.J. He probably told my lawyer to do what he thought best.'

'That's not why you want to disappear,' said Gerard.

'I became a grandmother and lost my way of life. It's crazy.'

'He has a past, of course,' said Gerard. He waited for her to answer. She stayed silent. 'Could be to do with that. Loss makes people a little crazy. We humans can't deal with it. The older tribes, they say, were here a long time ago and they understood it.'

'So, what did the lawyer say?'

He wrote a figure on a piece of paper and slid it across the table to her. She looked at it and slid it back. 'Tell the lawyer to tell my ex-partner that I came into it with nothing and I'll go out of it with nothing. There is nothing in this world that he could give me.'

Chapter 18

Mia turned the fan on in the Decision Chamber. 'If we take the coach north to the mountain it will cost a few hundred euros. I don't have it. I started making a bit today. Also, we should concentrate on Girona because that is most likely where the Grail Cup trail starts.' It was also where she would have a chance of seeing her lover of the past.

Belle said, 'I think the mountain is a good idea.'

Mia looked at Belle. 'Couldn't you pay for it?'

Belle didn't hesitate. 'Not right now.' The other women were indeed surprised. Cynthia said they would have to book the coach now because the numbers were increasing. Also, it took them straight from the spa to the mountain.

Belle sighed. 'It's not the best time for me. I don't have a buck.'

The women stared at her as though she was some strange animal. Mia kept thinking, 'God, make it more real.'

'They've locked down or closed off all my accounts. I was going to ask if I could go three ways with you in this room.'

'What the hell happened?' said Mia.

'A long story or the short version?'

Cynthia poured three drinks from the Ratifia bottle and added ice. 'With lemon?'

They drank in silence.

Belle felt much better in this room with these women. Of course, she would get money together. There was her father's bequest in Norway, his property and her own small careless accounts here and there across the world. I didn't see it coming, she told herself.

Belle moved another bed into the room and Jonas Boon moved into hers.

Belle had maybe half a day of feeling relief, then reality set in. Jasper Jay would never let this go.

His lawyers could do many things but when it came to the real stuff — deception, humiliation, fatal exposure, they had no solution. Jay would never get over this. As she lay again sleepless in the shared room, she could see his eyes darkened with revenge tunnelling their way towards her. You can always disappear? From those eyes?

Suddenly there were four in the Decision Chamber and Esmee, wearing a Chanel little black dress and Ferragamo shoes, sat at the small table. Even the green bow was gone and her hair up in a severe knot. She meant business. 'Let's get rid of the fear. The room is full of it. I am a hands-on healer and I will start with a mantra to say several times a day. Whoever sends me negative energy I send it back for God to judge. I do not want it.'

Cynthia said she didn't think it was applicable to her and then she thought better of that boast.

There were three practices that everyone seemed to like. Breathing into an imaginary coloured expanding ball, held between real lifted curving arms, known as 'Breathing the Balloon', was the favourite. In case anyone found it too slow or even boring Mia reminded them that sages across the globe could breathe so fine and calm it took 45 minutes to fill. As in this group it took five, they had something to think about. Sitting calm and hearing sounds far, near and internal was pleasing to do. The second was Ohm chanting in a circle, a recipient for healing in the middle. They liked practices that made them feel better. They did not like balancing or positions they did not have the flexibility to fully reach. Some found painting a still-life of rock and stone absorbing and could use it as a key to inner journeys leading to outer unknown spaces. They got their money's worth.

Belle took them walking and running. Cynthia sat and listened to their problems and gave sweet advice. She was always on their side. She would enclose them in her unconditional approval no matter what their crime and she'd bury the bodies for them if she had to. Grown men sat in front of her over the teacups and looked at her rosy cheeks, kind eyes and felt everything would be alright.

Mia started using a hypnotic exercise on all of them which worked directly on the subconscious. It had originated with a French doctor in the nineteenth century and got people well. 'Lie down, completely relax, eyes closed, say to yourself, "Every day in every way I'm getting better and better". Keep it going. You don't have to believe or visualize anything … it works.'

From there she took them into changing self talk, change the old patterns, change the way you think.

There still wasn't enough money.

Belle's statement, 'I have nothing,' coming from an uptown Monaco girl was perhaps the shock of the trip.

Then the day of Cynthia's return flight was in sight but it was as though it did not exist. No one mentioned it. Nor had she. She could not bear the thought of leaving. Mia went to Eric for advice.

'If you run the show and you take it on, you have to pay for the coach,' he said. He agreed the sessions she provided should be paid for. Girona would be less challenging than Mt Canigou and the hotel would give her a reduction. She asked if there was any news on The Cat. He said not. What did Gerard mean when he asked about The Cat's mother? He had no comment on that. Finally, how much could she ask for each session in Girona with sight-seeing included?

'I think I would concentrate on finding the Grail.' He paused. 'Take them to venues which have mystery as well as venues which might have the Grail. Get someone to give a talk on maps of the past. Cassini was the great map-maker in the seventeenth century. And get Belle to make some green organic smoothies.'

Belle heard the last suggestion as she crossed the grass to join them. 'I can make sorrel soup and blend vegetable quinoa.'

'How much profit?' said Eric. He laughed at her estimate and said for a group it was not much.

She laughed. 'I'll do it for passers-by with a copy of the Grail map as a napkin.'

Eric hugged her. 'You're my kind of girl.' He took a list from his pocket. 'This is how it goes. Some filming of the group here at the spa. I do it for nothing and they get prints. You can't get one buck out of Esmee, I'm afraid. How can anyone think she is rich when she's been

144

wearing that same green bow since the beginning of time etc. etc? Shereen will leave when the frozen lobster runs out. I've told her it's only just died and been put straight on ice. Hence the stiff look. I can collect something from her. And Ramon. Maggie is an unknown. Always is. I'll do the best I can. Lily won't pay. Ah, I'd forgotten Dick Topper.'

People always did.

'It's as though he is invisible. Magicians use number five. It hides them and their dealings. Maybe he is an actual magician.'

'He'll be good for a bit more.' Eric would arrange the bookings.

'Where does he get his money from?' Mia asked.

'From all over. He comes from Milton Keynes and works the circuits as a magician,' Eric replied. Mia asked if he was. 'No idea. You can be anything on these tours.'

They decided they'd leave for Girona the next day in the cool of the evening.

The Decision Chamber was aptly named and the best place to choose the next move. There were always 'next moves'. 'I think we should go on with the workshops if only because it's getting us into shape,' said Belle. 'We've got to think of ourselves.'

'What about the Grail?' said Cynthia.

'Well that too,' said Belle.

'Is there one?' Cynthia asked her.

'I don't see why not. They're all sort of running after the idea. Even Gerard knew that map was for real.'

'I wish I could go to Girona,' said Cynthia suddenly. 'I need a Grail to do that.'

'I knew this would happen,' said Belle. 'You've got too attached to this place.'

'Well, I have a bit.' Cynthia sat on a chair leaning forward, elbows on knees, palms taking the weight of her head in a yin position she had learned from the workshop. She was thinking of her kitchen floor in her green-belt home and her on it, washing the tiles with a cloth. And Jenny with the spa escape. 'You need it more than me.' And in return she got Ed. 'I've done everything for him,' she said aloud. 'The

145

bastard. Oh, and Jenny said, "What you need is a good lover and a sit in the sun." ' Then she thought of Joey's missed birthday. 'I have to go back.'

'Are you serious?' said Mia.

'Return ticket tomorrow.'

'We don't let a return ticket rule our lives,' said Belle. 'You can't go back. It's all just beginning. We can make this thing work.' She jumped across the bed on the way to comfort Cynthia. 'When did you last have time on your own? Just say you are staying on, recuperating after the bug.'

'The grandchildren. I missed Joey's birthday.'

'Ed and Jenny,' said Belle promptly.

They sat in silence.

'Let's ask the skull,' said Belle. 'And it's three minutes to dinner.'

Mia didn't have a return date. Belle had nowhere to return to.

'The walking and resting have done you good, Cynthia,' said Mia. 'Not to mention the little outings with your dining companion. What kind of magician is he? Maybe he could look at the Grail map.'

'Do you believe it?' said Cynthia.

Mia paused. 'There must be something.' She did believe it. She knew the territory. This place would have mysteries. She looked at Belle. 'You don't believe it.'

'No,' said Belle. 'But I wouldn't mind having it right now.' She told Cynthia to first phone the family then come and make some organic smoothies with Carlos. 'And I made the starter tonight. Sorrel soup.'

The card games raised pleasure as much as the food and had become a useful contrast to the metaphysical practises. They played to win and the games were silent and absorbing. Mia could lose herself in a game of Blackjack to the point where she forgot the problems. When would she be in good enough shape to come face to face with Sal Roca?

During the last night walk around the village in which Belle liked to make the women increase their speed — 'heel, toe, heel, toe, stretch calves' — she said she had asked Eva if she could have an audience with the skull. 'So, let's really push the limits and go around once more before midnight strikes.'

146

Neither Cynthia nor Mia wanted to even look at the skull. Eva explained it as an object made of mostly crystal which had been blessed and she could pick up its inclinations and even answers to people's questions. Mia said it was a relief the skull did not speak. She had imagined it alive like the lobsters Shereen demanded but did not get.

'There aren't many skulls around,' said Eric. 'They are exclusive and expensive.'

The skull wrapped in its blanket was already placed on the parlour card table and Eva said one person could come forward and ask the questions. Cynthia agreed Belle should take that role. Then Eva stood up and asked the others to leave and the last they saw was Belle bending over, gazing with welcome into the immovable eyes of the 'crystal sage'.

The women sat up rather than lying down to avoid giving in to sleep. Cynthia made tea with honey and opened the box of black chocolate. 'It contains sea salt and hardly any sugar. Oh, what does it matter? We can make anything sound what we want. Whatever the skull thinks, I still have to worry what Ed thinks.'

'That's what we haven't addressed enough in the workshops,' Mia realized. 'The wrong use of words. Worry. Let's change it. Positive. Replace worry.'

'Why?'

'It's a habit.'

They agreed the chocolate was wonderful. 'What do you really have to tell Ed? Think new thoughts.'

Cynthia tried. 'I don't know.'

'Replace "worry" with "no longer worry about what Ed thinks" or get on with my life. Or...'

'I'm not very good at that. Or meditation etc. But I see what you mean. We must also ask Belle about her situation. I was sort of hoping she would just come out with it.'

Belle opened the door softly but they were wide awake waiting.

'It's not a gimmick. It's a way of tuning in. She is psychic and by holding the skull sees things and gets answers.'

'That sounds better,' said Cynthia relieved.

'It's obviously the skull's attunement working through her. She said three grandmothers will go in search of the Grail.'

'But there's only two of us,' said Mia.

'I recently became number three.' The news jumped out of her.

Cynthia congratulated her warmly.

'You really don't look like it's possible,' said Mia.

'I wish,' said Belle. 'Of course, it's great. But there's always the two sides of everything. You know the silver lining one, well this is the opposite.'

Cynthia's mind filled with the horror of a deformed baby, a cot death. 'Anything I can do?' she asked softly.

'Yes, stay here. Let's find the Grail. I think we could all do with a little luck.'

Chapter 19

Maggie decided to eat the homemade jam as this was her last breakfast at the spa. Her cases were packed, bill paid, driver instructed to include a trip to the Dolmen in Romanya on the way to Girona no matter what the group had in mind. 'We'll leave at seven,' she told Eric. 'So we miss the evening traffic at eight.' Maggie liked the kale drink. 'Belle blends a good smoothie. One line gave her age away. Studio 54.'

'Yeah,' said Eric. 'It just takes one line.'

'Are you talking about Belle?' said Lily. 'What's happened to her?'

Maggie had a captive audience. 'She's probably 54. She's been 30 forever. Of course, J.J. knew.'

'You've lost me there,' said Ramon.

'The companion. They weren't married. But they lived together for years. In her situation that is living as though you're 20 years younger. It's hard work. You can't have an off day.'

'I don't think 20 years.' Eric laughed. 'Ten maybe. On a candid photo she's not bad.'

'She has Eric fooled and her plastic surgeon deserves a medal,' said Maggie.

'I don't see any surgery on that face,' said Ramon.

'Exactly,' said Maggie. 'He's very good whoever he is. But whatever packaging you manage, you are the age you are. You look a good 40 but your experience is a definite 60. You are your age.'

Ramon could not agree more.

'But you can get it better by what Mia's doing. The no sugar, exercise, calm mind, laughter. She's on the right track with the wrong people. The Lobster is "going to give her hell in Girona". There's no live lobsters in town. No fish market. Eric's checked.' Maggie turned to Ramon, 'Any Botox on Belle?'

'There's no sign. Nothing's lifted.' Ramon was struck by Belle's

149

perfect face. 'It's genetic. She looks more beautiful without makeup.' The others agreed.

'I photographed her right up close,' said Eric. 'In really unflattering light and whatever it is, she's got it.'

They sat silent enjoying the tortilla with onion and herbs. Eric said he could eat four eggs a day. Maggie asked for fresh coffee. Time passed. Finally, Lily had to ask what was so show-stopping.

Esmee said, 'What gives it away is you look at her and see a beautiful woman. Flawless. But she's not young. Close your eyes and see her. She's not 20. It's disconcerting. J.J. must have known but she was his trophy. Is it that which has upset him? He finds out ... what?'

Cynthia filled her plate from the buffet and joined them.

'Did she have little flings?' said Esmee.

'If she did, he will have known about them,' said Maggie. 'He couldn't have minded too much. For him it was all about youth. And I know why. Men want women to have the face of a four-year-old child. Simple as that. Smooth and nothing on it. Eighteen is already on the edge. So, women go to the surgeon and he listens to all the bullshit and already knows what he has to do. Make it look like four.'

Nobody contradicted Maggie.

'I take it we are talking about Belle's husband or partner,' said Cynthia.

'She deceived him. Took 15 years off her age.'

'It must be something else,' said Lily. 'She's an incredibly nice person.'

Cynthia knew whatever she did she must not mention the deadly word 'grandmother'. They did not know yet. She tried to change the subject but Lily wanted to know if Maggie had met J.J.

'Only in passing. The Lobster, Shereen, worked for him briefly. She's tops in IT. And she saw Belle in Washington. She made several trips to Washington. Maybe had a lover there. She must have had a horrid life. Because he is a nightmare. Tyrant. It's all the fountain of youth. Nothing is allowed to move on.'

'So, what's happened to Belle?' asked Cynthia.

'Amputation,' said Maggie. 'Especially at the bank.'

They were all shocked, each in a different way.

'So how did you find out?' said Cynthia.

'The Lobster. She's been around these machines and technology for too long. She talks like she's a human email.'

Eric laughed. 'Got that. No connection with the message. Just the message.'

'J.J. dumped wife of 15 years. So, watch out you grandmothers,' said Maggie.

Cynthia shivered. Not for herself. 'Let's go out and do the "Psychic Baptism". It sounds just what we need.'

Mia went to Maggie's room to challenge her. 'How could Cherie...'

'Shereen!' Maggie corrected her.

'...walk into this spa and know details of a scandal that may not even have...'

'It happened.' Maggie cut in. 'I agree it's a big world but a small place.'

'But how does she just walk into this unknown place in the middle of nowhere?' she insisted.

'You've seen the movie. Bogart said, "Of all the gin joints in the world why does she come into mine". *Casablanca*. There's a hundred thousand people in a stadium, all strangers and you run into the very person you've not seen for years, have thought about for even longer, have tried to locate and finally given up.'

'It happens. Shereen knew Lily at some point and followed her interest in Kelly Brooke. She met her with Deepak and even came on one of the groups. So, she came on this one late and didn't know Kelly Brooke was absent until she went to the coast. She decided to still drop in here and see Lily. She works for government. I know J.J.'s story. He was a very bright Princeton boy and people said charming and good natured. Went into one of the banks, then Wall St. Made a killing with a gamble on oil. He lost the wife he loved and his little girl in separate accidents within three months of each other.

When I met him some years later, he used to sit in my friend's kitchen in LA and the tears would just fall from his eyes at almost regular intervals. He wasn't crying. It was just the result of the trauma and bereavement. He had changed by then and was an

151

apprentice tyrant. Now he's the full thing, an arms dealer on a global level.'

'Can we keep this to ourselves and not spread it?'

'To who? The ones here know it. Everyone's heard of him.' Maggie paused. 'I don't think Belle cares if you ask me. She's a survivor. And she's got past whatever she thought she'd found with him.'

Later Mia went back to Maggie's room, just to check the rest of the story. 'Is this really why he got rid of her? 'Cos she was older than she'd said?'

'I'm sure it was because she'd been 15 years younger for a lot of years.'

She didn't see any reaction to suggest otherwise. But she still asked if there was something else.

'Like?'

'Another man? Another life?'

'Why don't you ask her?'

Mia took the group not outside as expected but into the main card room. 'The "Psychic Baptism" has been around for years,' she said. 'And to do it we need to be inside. Here it is. Take a sheet of paper, a pen and a candle.' She indicated the supply on the main table. 'Sit at a table of your choice, light the candle and decide who it is you have the most resentment for. Someone who left you, deceived you, hurt you, . . . could be years ago. Could be last week. Visualize this person and write him or her a letter outlining the resentment, hurt and pain. Write quickly, accusing that person. You did this, you did that. List the main betrayals. Do not reread your letter. Sign it and take it and your candle over to the sink.' She indicated the washroom. 'Burn the letter. Flush some of the ash down with cold water. Throw salt on the plug. There's a box already in there. This is an old Spanish custom. Salt kills off the anger and negative energies. Blow the candle out and go for a quick walk for two minutes around the garden. Breathe. Then find a place to sit and use one of the meditations. We will meet up in a circle one hour from now. You may feel emotional, you may not, but in a few days, you will feel lighter and freer. It's not a lobotomy. It's like after an operation. You remember the pain but you don't feel it anymore.'

152

Mia waited in the washroom, to clear the sink of ash and salt as they came in at five-minute intervals.

Cynthia would have written her letter about Ed. She wrote instead about J.J. and what he had done to Belle.

After lunch Maggie said, 'I want the Grail experience. I've had a good full life and compared with many, eventful. I've met the people I thought I wanted to meet. But there's something I've missed, or is missing? The spiritual experience of being with that stone, even in its proximity will make sense of the emptiness I often feel. I will be filled like some people are by religious belief.'

Lily said, 'I hate getting old. I hate old. I've missed young. Always had to be responsible. Writing that letter made me feel that.'

Mia said, 'Old age is a punishment for a crime I did not commit.'

Maggie laughed. 'Bette Davis said old age is not for sissies.'

Belle said, 'There are two happenings in my life that make me know I am going to be alright. I'll share them with you.' She moved to the chair at the top of the table. 'I was a kid when I arrived in the US with no visa or credit details or credentials. Just myself and a passport. I was 18. And the security officer liked my style, and looking me up and down he said, "One thing's sure. With your attitude you'll never starve in this country." And he let me through. And I knew then I could do it myself. Life. I didn't need anyone.' She paused. 'And the second—I took a boat out once into the middle of the ocean. Alone. It was pitch black. Just sea, stars, sky. And there were lights deep up there in the solar system, crossing pathways of momentary brilliance. A shooting star dashing downwards into the horizon. There's so much going on there. I sat in the darkness with just the sound of the water and gradually I understood the meaning of it all.'

'All?' asked Mia.

'Life. I hope I will never forget that night. And whatever happens I know I will be alright.'

Chapter 20

The three women shared the Girona hotel suite at a preferential rate. If they would take on two new guests who had arrived for the group they'd get 'daily menu' meals free. There was a completely different energy in Girona and Mia felt the city welcomed her back. Cynthia said she could feel this energy physically. It made her ankles swell, her eyelids puffy, and no amount of makeup would stay on her face. 'It's a very physical place,' she said and flopped onto the bed.

'It's all about the Grail now,' said Mia. 'You can feel our purpose has tightened.'

'I don't think I'm going to make it to the Grail. Not all that way up the mountain.'

'We've got time,' said Mia. 'Let's give it a few more days of preparation. We've booked in here for another five. We're going to visit the sites on the journey to the Grail. Palera and a village in the Pyrenees.'

Cynthia winced and kicked off her shoes. She looked like an oversized child about to throw a tantrum. 'I just want to go to the cinema.'

Mia was almost appalled. 'I hope you don't represent the rest of the group. I mean I've worked hard to...'

'Oh no.' Cynthia managed to sit up. 'I've loved every minute and I'm grateful. It's opened up a new world. I've changed. But if I could just spend this evening laid out watching television, especially old black and white movies, and do a bit of shopping. I've got to get things for the grandchildren. You know how it is.'

If only – chance would be a fine thing.

'And can we do a day at the sea?'

Mia looked at her spoilt friend flattened by age and childishness and decided to laugh. 'You are ace with the clients and their problems.'

'I feel for them. If listening helps, I'll do it, but I can't do that

154

mountain. If the skull says it has to be three grandmothers you will have to find another one. I am so tired. And is the Grail dangerous in itself? And all those who want to find it—they're not going to like three clapped out grandmothers crawling up a mountain.'

'But Cynthia, who says the Grail is up a mountain? Where has this idea come from?' Who had said it? She would like to know. For a moment it had sounded familiar.

Cynthia had no idea and she assumed they were going up the mountain to get the Grail. 'What else are we doing up there?'

'We are going to dance across mountain peaks in a spiritual conquest. We claim the mountain.' That's what Mia had understood. 'Belle first produced the plan as a symbol of victory over ourselves.' But that did not mean the precious stone or metal was there. Or was it? Confused she got ready for the fitness assessment with Mercedes, her friend from the old days. Cynthia was applying more makeup. 'You are going out with Dick Topper for dinner, aren't you?' she realized.

'Yes, we're going to Can Xifre in the countryside. It has its own farm. The food is to die for. The patron makes her own organic lemonade and fig marmalade. Not only that, I've asked him to work some magic with the map.'

'But we should all be on that,' said Mia firmly.

'What? The whole group?'

And then Mia understood this was the moment of decision. There were two groups. The 'Maggie' group and the 'three grandmothers'.

'Just us.' Mia decided.

'And Belle?'

'Definitely. If you think I can get you up a mountain alone then you do need a night at the cinema.'

'You feel alright with her, don't you? It could be the Hollywood thing you share. I envy you because you've done something with your life. You've gone out there and really tried and had exhibitions.'

'People have a short memory. Over the years very few movie stars are remembered let alone artists. Time wipes you out.'

'You're a good teacher. I've not done anything. It's too late.'

Mia sat down and really listened. Her second husband always said she was an active listener and that was a valuable asset. She could always be a shrink if things got that bad.

'I'm just trapped in this body and all I feel is heavy.' Cynthia spoke softly. 'And one day when we were doing a little running, I began to feel light as if I could just jump up and stay up. It was a good feeling. I felt as I really should be.'

Mia almost suggested breathing deeply and letting it all go and — she could suggest a lot of things — she just sat there not speaking.

'So, I suppose I can help if I get Dick Topper to have a look at the map.' Cynthia's energy had veered off from trouble. Mia could speak now.

'What sort of magician is he?'

'Events. He's an Ace-up-the-sleeve kind. He gets bookings. And runs a magic circle.'

'Does he have a job, as in pay-packet?'

'He inherited a couple of businesses. Grandfather was in the furniture trade and did well. Dick never wanted any of that. He was sent to the right schools but he's really keen on transformation. I think if we use his skills in locating the Grail, he should come with us.'

That was something that would not happen. Imagining Belle's face hearing that idea made Mia laugh. She had to work on Cynthia very hard to get her down to the fitness assessment with Mercedes.

Mercedes Salvat had a dry approach, straight-faced and found people's ideas of how they could look and what they could do so comic that if she'd reacted to it, she'd have been out of a job years ago. She was tested yet again when Belle said, 'I want you to get us up a mountain.'

Mercedes stayed straight-faced but her eyes were full of laughter. 'All of you?'

'Can you get us fit enough to climb?'

'Then we get in the gym. The whole group at the hotel as well?'

'No,' said Mia. 'Just us three.'

Mercedes had her own gym and ran a service of private trainers. She quickly tested the women. Mia needed more strength and tone, especially her legs. Her breathing could be better. More protein. Cynthia, out of the question. Carrying too much weight. 'Could get

156

you up a hill. You are basically strong. And you have stamina. You are just protecting yourself with all that flesh.'

'Am I?' said Cynthia.

'It's an inside job. Focus your mind. Change your thoughts. Slow build up in exercise.'

Belle—'You can climb any mountain any time.'

They agreed to start in the gym first thing the following morning.

Mia walked with Mercedes to the iron bridge. 'One question. Is Sal Roca around? You remember him?'

How she hoped Mercedes did.

'He's around. But I don't mix with that set. Too up the ladder for me. But he's wonderful. How else could he be?'

'Do you ... see him?'

'I run into him now and then. He's the same. A poet of life. I haven't seen him lately now you mention it. But there's a few changes in town.'

'Like?'

'Let's call it acquisitions.' She winked. 'I'll do my best, my friend, for you.'

After a substantial dinner the reduced group sat on the paseo. Cynthia and Dick Topper were having their own dinner. Shereen, lobster-less, had stayed in her room. Eva and the skull were visiting friends and Belle was sorting out a money transaction in Western Union. Maggie said, 'Belle is totally brave. I so approve of her. Apparently, she told J.J., "I came in with nothing. I go out with nothing. There's nothing you have that I want." She should have got a settlement agreement in the first year. It's been hard work. She had to be "on" all the time and now he won't give her a dime. Today's girls would ask for theirs upfront. They're not so naive. They've been to school and want a share of things, a percentage of assets. These trophy girls like Belle last for five years max. She did 20.'

Esmee said he wasn't with her all the time.

'He wasn't with anyone all the time. He travelled. He's global,' said Maggie.

'She must have played a close hand,' said Esmee. 'It must be more than a date of birth. Age is just a number.'

Mia thought of the man in the photo. Perhaps he was the 'more'.

'I remember Clifford Odets before he died writing his own eulogy,' said Maggie. She asked Mia if she remembered him.

'He was a wonderful screenwriter and playwright,' she replied. *Sweet smell of success*, is my favourite film.'

'Brilliant,' Eric agreed. 'He was the golden boy. What was his eulogy?'

Maggie knew it by heart. 'That miserable patch of events, that melange of nothing. While you were looking ahead for something to happen. That was it. That was life. You lived it.'

Vicky Smart walked to the reception with intent and carried her luggage. No dust settled on this newcomer and she meant business. Mia only noticed her because she was like a conservative version of Cynthia. She was a good 60 going on 70 and knew what she wanted. And got it. She was here for transformation. She wanted her life changed and refuelled. Rebirth came next. She had read Kelly Brooke and it could be done. She was torn between domestic life and freedom. Why did she want to be free? Her husband asked that enough. She needed to explore and study 'The Meaning', 'The Reason', 'The Point'. She had absorbed Kelly Brooke, her interviews, her books, to the extent she could quote whole passages.

'I want to speak to Miss Brooke,' she told reception.

'Why?' Eric happened to be getting money changed for Maggie. His question was automatic and a touch stressed.

Vicky wanted to be changed and enlightened by the teacher's visionary promise. It got worse. She wanted to devote her life to Kelly Brooke.

Eric said later it made him see the slippery divinity in a different light. For 10 days she had been an excruciating absence that had drained him of all goodwill, respect, even the wish to ever see her again.

'I want to go with her into "The chemical wedding" which only those truly ready can even approach. I am ready.' This woman had travelled two days by car from Wales which had heightened her nervous system and expectations. 'I just want to thank her and say she has changed my life as she has hundreds of others.'

'Undoubtedly,' said Eric. 'Have you booked?' How he prayed she hadn't. She had booked. 'You could simply write her a note expressing this gratitude. I can make sure she gets it.' He thought for a moment the slippery one could actually be dead. He realized he could be cracking up. He had spent hours with these women sorting out their miserable self-esteem or mountain-high egos and now this fervent person wanted to open it all up again. No painting and drama here with chairs flying. Just the real thing.

'I've worked daily to get fit to get up that mountain,' she said eagerly.

'Have you indeed?' And his mind filled up with the vision of a long-wet corpse. Maybe he was turning into a murderer of women. He threw Maggie's money on the floor. For once he was at a total loss. She was like her name 'Smart' and there was no sense 'fudging the issue' as Cynthia liked to say. Money transactions forgotten he helped her to her room and got reception to send tea and snacks. She told him she would come down when she was prepared to meet Kelly. Meditation and chanting had to precede everything, didn't they? He was thinking, if Mia was younger, he'd run away with her from all this and never stop.

Eric stood at the top of the third flight of stairs. Why hadn't he gone to the lift? He was thinking about his life which was not his choice, either the thought or the life. He thought about the cost on his nerves travelling with Maggie, the glue of her promises that kept him stuck fulfilling her needs. The favourite, the promise of meeting the famous and the super-rich or, the illustrious career he'd have as a cameraman, how talented he was — so obvious to everyone. The more these considerations crossed his mind, the more his body tipped to the diagonal position from which a fall was inevitable. He straightened up sharp. 'Jesus! It must be the humidity.' But the talent she always talked about was there before they met. He was all bright with promise in the Marty days and the long short he did with Jack up in the actor's Mulholland kitchen with its old olive-green fridge. The Bert Schneider time — he was a kid then and Bert said he had 'it' and he was a guy that recognized 'it'. Would Maggie give him the backing she'd talked about? The trouble was her backing did not sound like Marty's backing. Or Schneider's. His face was running with sweat. Hands wet too and trying to hold on. Edge back to the safety of the lift.

Then Vicky Smart's door opened. 'Could you get me a towel?'

He turned and looked at her. She and her towels had nothing to do with his life. 'What do you actually want?' Women asking him for room items in a hotel usually ended with a further item he could not alas give.

'Want? What do you mean?'

Now an idea occurred that dried his skin and straightened his back. He was considering passing off Mia in sunglasses and a floppy hat as the 'Mistress of Divine'. Kelly rarely had a direct camera shot out in public. Her PR was blurred and grainy. She'd said it added to the mystery. Vicky stayed correctly in her doorway. 'I want to go far out into the ocean and see it all as it really is. That's when you look up and understand and hear the sounds you never hear.'

Her words were familiar. Hadn't Belle said something similar? Was there such a thing as synchronicity?

'You could do that. Take a boat and just go so you're beyond all this, yourself and your needs. I think we are all spirit having a human experience.'

He liked that. He felt much better and ran down the stairs.

'A large size towel,' she shouted after him. And added, 'Please.'

Outside in the paseo the group had not one clue how to deal with the situation. They agreed the money had to be repaid. For her to join them now would be an intrusion. Eric said again she meant business and was a true dedicated student. She was too smart for the kind of thing they did, and that gave him a table full of enemies. He tried to justify the insult.

'Don't be so silly,' said Maggie. 'She's after the Grail, same as everyone else.'

Vicky Smart living up to her name joined them too quickly, showered and well turned out. She was surprised Kelly Brooke was not at the table.

160

'Yes, we've all been through that,' said Mia.

Vicky had an open manner, a warm smile and was used to people. 'Thank God she's friendly,' said Mia softly and began the first sentence of the version of Ms Brooke's absence and unlikely return. 'So, we've not had anyone to deliver her texts and teachings.'

'I can do it,' said Vicky suddenly.

Mia said her offer was incredibly nice but they had gone beyond that point of revelation.

'Academia,' corrected Maggie.

'And we're definitely somewhere else.'

Questions followed. Sufficient answers did not. Vicky Smart decided something must have happened. There were no answers anymore. Then Vicky made a sudden decision. 'She's been kidnapped by elementals.' It was no sillier than anything else and everyone stayed silent. The truth was the group had jelled together. Even the Lobster had a place.

'We can't just start again,' said Eric. 'But you are welcome to...' What it was nobody would know as Maggie kicked Eric under the table.

'I am very much into physics and space exploration. I think Ms Brooke has opened up some form of de-centralized space exploration which is also aligned with spirituality. I have met serious men from The States.' And she named them. And Maggie said they were serious. 'This is where Kelly's work is leading.' Vicky became over engaged and dozens of words followed and Mia thought she was going to faint.

Lily's eyes had begun to shine. 'This is like the old days. I'm so glad you've come. The ones still on the coast will love you.'

'Happy to help. I think you should consider the CIA. Have they taken Kelly?'

'I think we have other issues now,' said Mia. 'But perhaps you could do — something.'

'Happy to. I can give a talk on Kelly's direction and where it fits in with Elon Musk.'

And then they heard the unmistakeable sound of Gerard coming towards them.

161

Eric quickly took the too-new arrival for a view from the bridge. Later they all agreed Vicky was the real thing and somehow brought new blood in but the old dark blood of that group was sort of done for. 'Let's give her The Lobster,' said Eric. 'They've probably got the same IQ level.'

Lily said, 'I'll take her.'

Like all of them Vicky had decisions to make. Her husband, retired, now needed her company. She wanted to be free to explore. She was 74 and needed to do it now or never. She described herself as a onetime translator in German turned into a domestic earth goddess. Maggie laughed longer than usual on that one. Vicky had tried Glastonbury but it wasn't deep enough. She wanted the real thing. She wanted Kelly. Kelly would know what Vicky should do. 'As long as she doesn't want the Grail,' said Maggie. 'What about the husband?'

'Oh, he's into boats. Let her give a talk,' said Eric.

'I've been through too much for anymore,' said Mia.

'Ditto,' said Belle.

Gerard accepted a drink and joined the paseo table. He said there was no actual news about The Cat but it was likely she was still in the area. 'Alive?' said Eric. 'I mean I hope so.'

'I hear you're climbing a mountain,' said Gerard.

'Not at all,' said Mia. News certainly got around. Mercedes? Room bugged?

'Of course, we are,' said Maggie.

'Which one?'

'It's not decided yet,' said Mia quickly.

'Canigou,' said Maggie. 'Of course.'

'Of course,' Gerard agreed.

A young woman just in from Boston and massively jet lagged came to the table looking again for Cynthia. 'Is this place Girona?' Jonas Boon sat alone waiting to see Cynthia. Shereen came onto the paseo and said she was front of the queue for Cynthia.

'Thank God I don't have to deal with them,' said Maggie.

'Yet,' said Eric. 'The night is still young.'

Dick Topper wrote numbers on a sheet of paper as he looked at the map from all sides. Quickly he turned the numbers into equations as Cynthia held the torch. They were sitting in a garden in the dark in the old quarter. Dick Topper turned the map until it spun — and was it the torch light that gave the impression the map lifted off the ground and fluttered back down? It now faced another direction and he pointed towards Canigou. 'North-West.' When he was working, he was focused and lost his ill-at-ease, not-quite-present attitude. Adding the numbers now he asked for Mia's birth date. She said the day and month but not the year.

'I need it,' he said. 'And we will get something. You are a sensitive and you hold information. Can I have your year of birth?'

'Give him the right one,' said Belle. 'I always thought you were at least 80 so surprise me.'

Mia said her age.

'Not bad,' said Cynthia. 'You've looked after yourself.'

Dick Topper wasn't interested in the women's discussion. He turned the map so it was upside down and drew on his sheet of numbers another design. It was the graffiti image Mia had seen on the wall in the old quarter the day she gave her first talk. She was amazed. 'It's a demonic face.'

Dick Topper agreed. Cynthia said she had thought it was a flower arrangement. 'That's to protect it,' said Dick Topper. 'Only a few who have worked this stuff could read that correctly. Let's go and look at the place where you saw it.'

Belle wanted to know what it meant.

'It's a number five. A pentagram. And five is the "invisible". It keeps things unseen. Magicians like number five.'

'He's got another side to him,' Belle said quietly to Mia. 'Let's keep it quiet about the mountain.'

Some things were too late. Mia found the wall near the Arc Bar where the graffiti had been. He ran his hand over the stone. 'It's active,' he said.

'Meaning?' asked Belle.

'It's used by further dimensions than ours.'

'To do what?'

'Perhaps to give messages,' he said. He took her hand without asking and placed it on the wall. 'It's not bad or dangerous. It just protects what's there.'

When they got back to the hotel the receptionist told Mia a woman had called her several times. 'She'll ring back.'

That night Mia could only think of Sal Roca. There was no question of sleep. He used to offer her everything she wanted. When the time was right.

She remembered the winter journey to the south. Getting the local train at Alicante at night. There was a small, country station full of blossom and they had got off to wait for the midnight train to Malaga. It was deserted and gas lamps blown by the wind cast huge shadows along the stone wall. There were peeling advertisements years old. The air was warm and scented. Orange blossom and mimosa grew on the platform of this station which was hardly used anymore. Men played cards in the bar and spoke roughly, in gusts. The wind was loud and the trees were swished together, sweeping furious against the scudding sky — stars and cloud and trees all jumbled by the wind. They could be in another time, that's what Sal Roca said. There was a presence, a suggestion of something in the wind. They were linked up with the past and she'd felt that before with him. She had swung in a tree and happiness made her do things she wouldn't normally think of. He held her legs, kissed her stomach, lifted her down. He picked a spray of bloom and presented it to her formally. Solitary bells were jangled by the wind.

There had been a presence on that station. It filled her with longing, with yearning for things she half understood, half believed could exist. He was affected by it. His gestures were ritualized — the handing of the blossom, the way he kissed her hand. She had led him into the bar. She had to move, to go inside, because out there on the platform, the feeling was overwhelming. It was as though the sky opened up and all the secrets, the mysteries were about to be revealed. But she kept her head down humbly and escaped among people in the bar. The glorious unknown daunted her as much as horror did.

164

Everyone in the bar had looked up as she came in. She was covered with white blossom.

'Like a bride,' said the man behind the bar.

'Radiant. And so young.'

They thought she was 16. She had just passed her twenty-fourth birthday. Ecstatic moments came off Sal Roca. Like sparks. Sometimes they took form, were gracious, filled an hour.

The spray of white blossom quivered on the iron-wrought, marble top table. It contained all newness and innocence. When Sal Roca went to the counter, a drunk Guardia Civil officer came across to her table and took the flower. She got up, went to his table, and took it back.

Everyone was silent. They thought she'd behaved dangerously. Sal Roca laughed, but not so as anyone would notice. 'My God, you deprive a policeman of pleasure. They put you in the prison for that here.'

She would have died for that blossom.

Chapter 21

Just Belle and Mia turned up for the early morning session at the gym. Mercedes had them work full out for 20 minutes and Mia lay on the floor without even stretching. It was a struggle to get her breathing satisfactorily. Mercedes gave her a warm tea with mineral salts and lay cold wet cloths on her forehead, neck and feet. She removed one and rubbed the area with warmth from a hot stone, then put the cold cloth back on and hot stone massage on her knees. 'I bet you've not worked out like that for a while,' said Mercedes.

Mia agreed she hadn't and when her heart was still racing, felt uneasy. 'I hope I'm alright.'

'You are.' Belle took her hand. 'You just reached your limits.'

Mercedes rolled her to and fro in a Feldenkrais calming exercise but it took longer to get normal than to reach the limits. Mercedes said she was fine now but to get herself a check-up when she got home. 'Nothing to worry about.' Mia agreed but she wouldn't go near those limits again.

Mercedes walked, her arm linked with Mia, across the paseo for breakfast. 'We're both getting on,' she said. 'You're bound to get something at our age. It's just a question of what.'

Mia asked if she knew Gerard. She was sure she did. He worked in security.

'What about The Cat?' said Belle.

No luck there. Too many people pass through the old city these days. 'All these groups or movies or reportage. We're like a new extinct culture.'

Mia felt too upset to eat much. Swallowing was the problem. She could feel her pulse beat hard way down in her feet. That's how it felt. She'd be doing a low mountain with Cynthia.

Belle and Mercedes discussed products and fitness and Mia was busy in her own thoughts. You're born and life's all about the denial of death. And then you get old and it has to be about the acceptance

166

of death. She promised herself and God if she got through this, whatever it was, she would walk along the coast blessing every beloved site she passed. 'How old is Sal Roca, now?' she asked.

Mercedes heard her. 'In his eighties. But on top of things.' She stopped and Mia thought she could have said more but chose not to.

When Belle left to get ready for the day Mia asked about the old time, the old friends.

'It's changing here. The rich have moved in.'

'Seriously rich?'

Mercedes nodded.

'Is that what you meant about acquisitions?'

'They've bought Mt O. Just outside Girona and you've passed it a million times, going north, a castle on top, a small hamlet. People here don't like it because it's where the political prisoners were kept during and after the Civil War. They were kept in the caves.'

Of course. Mia remembered the coach journey to the spa and the driver saying, 'Bad atmosphere.'

'It's exclusive?' she asked Mercedes.

'Completely exclusive. They call it "Paradise—The Rich on The Hill".'

'What do they do up there?'

'Have a celebrated life. Helicopters in and out. Some say they're doing voyages to Venus. An Indian guru is up there now.'

'What was it before?'

'An abandoned castle.'

'So why the interest?'

'It's got special dynamics, pathways through space, portals. They are using it to find out how to travel in time. There must be something in it because these people are serious and from all over the world.'

Mia asked her what she really thought was there.

'People say some documents about the past. Maybe from other spheres. But paradise is obviously part of it. It's absolutely wondrous—fountains, gardens, pools, going down the back of the hill. The music is amazing and sometimes you can hear it down here carried by the mountain wind. And they've got world-class artworks, a master chef, A-list visitors.'

'Shangri La?'

'Sort of.'

'*Citizen Kane*. Remember the film?' And she wondered if Belle's former partner was one of the global entrepreneurs. 'Have you been up there?' Mia suddenly felt excited. A lot better.

'Only to the no admittance door.' Mercedes had to go for her next client and Mia forgot to ask who owned it.

Belle suddenly felt down, unusual for her. She hadn't wanted to leave the spa. He would never look for her there. He would think she was lying low in Paris or New York. He would never give up till he found her.

'Why don't you tell him like you've told us?' said Cynthia.

'He does not talk.'

'So, what does he do?'

'Reacts.'

There was a pause while they each decided what that could mean. Then Cynthia said she should tell the man in the photograph. 'He looks as though he would look after you. '

'I'd never involve him in this.'

'But you love him.'

'Exactly.'

The group visit to Palera which included the new members had to be delayed because one of Cynthia's devotees was lost and another wanted her money back. A third had luggage lost at the airport. Mia brought them water and lemons.

'Good thinking,' said Ramon. 'This air is a little too over-breathed.'

Mia asked if Lily would like to take part in a psycho-drama workshop. They were starting on the patio. It might be helpful.

'I've got nothing against you,' was her answer. 'But I'd rather work with Vicky. She can reach into dark space. Works with particles.'

Ramon with a movement of his eyes indicated he would be better dealing with this alone.

The tables on the paseo were moved into the shade as Cynthia was trying to deal with the jet-lagged woman from Boston who not having a room put aside for her, had spent the night lying in a garden in the old part. She was covered in grass and earth, soaked in sweat, tears and had no money, and somewhere along the desolate route she had lost her belongings.

'What can we do for you first?' said Mia. 'Breakfast?' The woman wanted to take a shower and Cynthia thought Belle wouldn't mind if she got cleaned up in the suite. Their hearts were in the right place but the woman, Lola le Baye, in the state she was in, had no spacial or bodily awareness and her management of the shower went badly and the bathroom was flooded and there seemed no way to turn off the tap. Water had passed through to the ceiling below. In the meantime, Lola had simply laid down helpless, wet and naked on Belle's bed and collapsed into sleep.

Jonas Boon wanted to finish his list of domestic problems and get Cynthia's 'solid advice. Nothing whimsical there.'

Another client who Cynthia had mistaken as a hotel guest came limping into view. She was dangerously furious. 'When I booked you didn't tell me there were cobbles. The streets are cobbled. I want my money back and ticket refunded.' Cynthia managed to find a cane for her to use and sent for Ramon to check her limping leg. 'I am completely out of balance,' said the woman.

'True,' said Maggie.

Cynthia helped the woman to sit on a pile of cushions and offered her water.

'Forget that,' said Maggie. 'Give her a Ratifia.'

Eventually the group were established on the hotel patio for the final psycho-drama session.

Mia invited Belle to sit on a stool and tell a story. She talked about loss and freedom. She was going to have to let go of the Lamborghini. Gerard was selling it for her that morning. She would have a less exuberant car but she needed the money. Did she experience loss? 'At first. But then I realized I was free.'

'Free?' said Shereen. 'Are you mad?'

'Would you like to take over her role?' said Mia.

'And do what?'

'Say how you feel about selling your Lamborghini.'

Belle got off the stool and indicated Shereen take her place. 'But she isn't selling it herself. Gerard is doing it. She always gets a man to do everything for her.'

There was a curious noise. It was Lily sobbing at the injustice of her loveless life. She would never have a man. It was too late. Ramon held her lovingly.

'How do you feel about that?' said Mia. 'Not having a man?'

Belle got back on the stool. 'Great. I haven't got one. The freedom is massive. I am going to climb a mountain and dance in the sky.'

The storm kept everyone inside and Eric took their minds off the still-delayed visit to Palera by talking about the Grail. Gerard decided to join them.

'OK. The Grail is very old. It's not from hereabouts. Holds truth from beyond our planet. It's linked with Venus and could well have associations with Lucifer who is said to have landed here on earth by the frontier with France over five thousand years ago. He was known as the Child of Light and brought us spirituality, evolvement, healing, wisdom, freedom of will, intuition. The locals here have always worshipped "The Child of Light". There have been celebrations of his existence and his light. There is a luciferic guild of light in the care of the shoemaker's guild. The Grail Cup is kept by an ancient society here in this area. Why is it kept out of our reach? Because we are not ready for it.'

And then Mia remembered many years ago Sal Roca told her about the stone beyond price which lifts us to a higher level.

'When will we see it?' she had asked Sal Roca.

'When we are ready. When the world is in a more optimistic state.' This didn't happen it seemed because the last time she enquired about the stone she was told many had sought it, to use it for their own purposes. 'In the wrong hands it would plunge the world into a catastrophic darkness,' he concluded.

Was this the Grail?

'I've heard over the years that it's looked after by elementals; they are beings and energies that have been here for thousands of years. Also,

170

people say that certain rhythms are used to locate the stone. It has a sound,' said Gerard.

'The hand that rocks the cradle rules the world,' said Belle.

Mia was called to reception and they said a woman was on the phone. Expecting Mercedes, she took the call. The woman's voice was deep and rough and not without humour. 'How are you getting on?'

Mia, not sure, did not answer.

'I can't face it frankly. They are too much trouble,' said the woman.

'Who? The Catalans?'

'No, you lot. The groups. Tell them to get a life.'

'Maybe we'll do it,' said Mia.

'I hear you found a few things. Be careful. It's not what it seems.'

After a pause Mia asked Kelly Brooke what she wanted.

'Safety.' She hung up.

Eric was waiting for her and said some of the group were getting bored.

'Try taking them on another sightseeing trip,' she said.

Firstly, she wrote down what the caller had said as best she could as her memory was apt to falter under strain. 'Safety'. That was the word. Also, the caller had heard Mia had discovered a few things and she seemed to be curious. That was what the call was about. Also, she had been the one to hang up. Mia would have asked questions but exactly which ones she wasn't sure. The call was completely unexpected. Also, was it her? What kind of voice did the woman have? A mongrel accent, bits of everything from everywhere. Her mood was not appealing.

She asked Lily how The Cat sounded.

'Sounded?'

'Her voice. What sort?'

'You really notice her. The energy, the expression, the aura, her colours. Her voice is ordinary.'

'U.S.?'

'A bit. You should ask the girls on the coast. The ones who do the radio show. She's . . .'

'Please don't say magical.' Mia went straight to reception and asked the girl if she recognized the caller's voice.

171

'A woman. Not Spanish. Could be Ms Brooke. It's her emotional content and personality that comes through.'

In that case Ms Brooke sounded down and dreary.

Belle called Gerard and the grandmothers met him across the iron bridge at a cafe in the Ramblas.

'Do you think she's following you?' said Gerard. 'If so, she'll know wherever you go. A dark corner cafe won't make any difference.'

'You do know what she looks like?'

'I do and she's not in the vicinity. I didn't suggest meeting in the cafes near the hotel because the others will join in. Or want to know what is said,' said Gerard.

'They all want the Grail,' said Mia.

'You'd better hurry up. Get Mercedes to bounce up those muscles.'

'So, it is up? As in mountain?'

'Of course. It wouldn't be underground. That would be unsuitable. Earth, movements, floods, rodents. This is an exalted object.' He turned to Mia. 'So, what did the caller say?'

'Do you remember her voice?' she asked him.

'I remember her speech patterns. Yes.'

Mia related as best she could the short content.

'Safety? So, you think she's suggesting you are in danger because of what you seek? She's trying to dissuade you from seeking further.'

'Are you looking for the Grail, Gerard?' said Cynthia.

'No but a lot of people are.' He finished his coffee and stood up. 'I have to go to work.' He put a hand on Mia's shoulder. 'She just tried to put you off. If you get another call ask someone to listen in. Nothing to worry about.'

They watched him walk up the Ramblas to his car. Mia said, 'There's a boy who doesn't have too many problems.'

'You don't think he took you seriously?' said Belle.

'What do you think?'

'My money's on a mountain but we need more to go on. Let's get to work on Dick Topper. Let's buy him a spectacular dinner.'

'Shall we do this Grail search?' said Mia. 'Is it safe?' She had the feeling The Cat was watching her. Someone was.

After the gym session she asked if she could speak to Mercedes alone. She suggested a cold drink in the Plaza Independencia Square lined with cafes and restaurants on all sides.

She told Mercedes of her concerns about The Cat and the Grail and admitted she did not know what she was really into. 'I've sort of ended up running the group.'

'What are you really here for?' Mercedes asked.

'This was a place where I was happy.' Then she said a lot more about her life than she intended. 'I have to keep going so I don't think about all this normally. "Things coming to an end". I'm just aware of time, as in maybe there's not much. I did want to see Sal Roca. One more time. I've never forgotten him.'

Mercedes took her hand and said something would be arranged. 'Let's concentrate on that and take it easy with mountain climbing.'

When Mia left, Mercedes went in search of Ramon. She mentioned her doubts about the painter's health. He agreed and said he would try again to take some action.

After Dick Topper, by using a basalt pendulum, indicated the direction of the Grail, the grandmothers went back to the 'Decision Chamber' and made a plan.

Cynthia asked if they really wanted to do this. Dick had not said 'up'. He had just said a direction.

It was a race, of that Mia was convinced. 'The Cat is watching us so she can follow us and take whatever it is. She won't want to lose all this that she's uncovered. Obviously, she's been discouraged and hopes we'll do the work for her.'

'What about the grandchildren?' said Cynthia.

'It's a challenge for us to work through what is coming for all of us. Let's go through to the summit and conquer death. It's an adventure. Let's go now and get the right walking shoes. We can't do much in flip-flops,' said Belle.

'I keep thinking of my grandson, Joey,' said Cynthia. 'The letter-writing baptism must have opened me up. I know what I want to do. Listening to people has given me that idea. No, I'm not going to study at my age. Psychotherapy practice is out. But it's so important to listen to people and to hug them. People don't touch anymore. I've

173

learnt that from the ones here. Lily said I was the first person to touch her in a week.' She paused. 'So, I'll do a listening and helping service. I've got the time now. Never thought I'd say that.'

'What about Ed?'

'She'll never leave Ed,' said Belle.

Cynthia wasn't sure. 'I think I have to accept him. But I need to have more fun. This trip has shown me that. And have fun with the children.'

'I'm ready for adventure,' said Belle. 'I would've liked to have been a real mother to my son. That's a hell of a regret. But I've learned something with our groups. I've got to be honest. And part of that is knowing where I belong. And it's not on the French Riviera.'

Mia asked if she'd try and see her son.

'He's become the sort of person he is, based in Washington. And not bad at that. All because I got him there. Right now, that person is dealing with something men don't like—feelings. My actual life has made him angry and afraid. I hope he and I do build something together. And of course, I would like to be part of the grandchild's life. As I'm saying it, I know it's bullshit. It won't happen. I will write him a letter and say I'd love to see him and his family.'

'Will you go to the man in the photo?' said Cynthia.

'I'm too old. There comes a point when you give that sort of thing up. I want to be free and free of my needs.'

'What does he do?' asked Cynthia.

'Astrophysics. He's good. He's also made money. Pass, on any more on that subject.' And for a terrible moment she thought she was going to cry.

Chapter 22

Gerard showed up driving along the paseo and beckoned to Mia who sat drinking coffee and enjoying the Blue Hour. He called to her to join him and opened the door. She thought he meant Belle.

'He means you,' said Belle.

She went across to the car to see what he wanted. He told her to get in and he sped out of Girona and she asked where they were going.

'Let's try Paradise.' He left the main road going north and turned towards the high hill. He turned on the car stereo and she remembered the French music.

'Gilbert Becaud,' she said. 'Haven't heard that for years. *Un Jour Tu Verras.*' They sang together along with Becaud. The road wound round the steep hill and the journey took much longer than she imagined. At one point he stopped and pointed to the view stretching as far as the sea and further north the French coast.

'Why am I going up here?'

'Someone said you should see it. You were here in Girona years ago and you did a lot for the Cabala centre and other things. Maybe the city owes you something.'

'Who is someone?' She hoped she kept the expectation out of her voice.

'Mercedes Salvat.'

They got back in the car and after 20 minutes of steep curving road arrived at a group of buildings with security gates and an armed guard with dogs. Recognizing Gerard, the guard pressed the button and the electronic gate opened. Gerard shared a joke in Catalan with the guard as they passed. Ahead a further steeper road.

'Thank God we didn't walk it,' she said.

'If you walk you come from the other side. The caves are there.'

'Is it easier?'

'It's worse.'

'Why go there?'

175

'Because that's the way you do it. Cars come this way. Most people go to Paradise by helicopter.'

She could hear dance music from the fifties. The car jolted to the top of the hill and here was Paradise. Everything was in complete darkness. He turned off the engine and said he was glad the car had good suspension.

'That music. It's from the fifties. Is this a gala?'

'Could be,' he said. And they got out.

A guard approached and Gerard handed over his keys so the vehicle could be parked for him. The large building was dark and closed over like a mollusc. Not one thing was visible except the huge mollusc shell.

'It's covered like that so it can't be seen from above.' Was he trying to reassure her? 'Nothing visible from above or below. Nothing there. Nothing to worry about. Nothing to climb a mountain for.'

Nearby a church bell tolled. She could see its dim shape.

'Was this place the castle?' She realized she was whispering.

'It is. It's just covered over at night.'

For a moment the church seemed to be lit up with silver stripes but it was simply a security vehicle passing overhead. The American dance music, *Only You*, seemed louder. She could hear laughter and the clink of glasses. She said she wasn't dressed for a party. Gerard did not seem totally at ease as he cleared his throat twice.

'How do we go in, Gerard? You have been here before?'

'You go in,' he said. 'I'm waiting for you here.' He went towards the mollusc and a grand door opened. Gerard pushed her gently, 'Shangri-La they say.'

The man at the door was difficult to see but the gloved hand beckoned her in.

The auditorium was huge, brilliant and elegantly filled. The live dance band played at the far end and the lighting changed smoothly from pink to gold to mauve in a manner that was hypnotic and perhaps designed to change thoughts. Of that she was sure. She turned to say a few words to the man who had opened the door but he was not there. It seemed she was on her own. 'Who would have thought under the mollusc there is so much light, life and celebration.' It seemed she was talking. But to who? People, excellently dressed, danced, changed partners, joined other groups. She walked as though in another reality. But there was nothing to worry about here. Splendour. Finesse. Elegance. Perfection. Splendid chandeliers. Some of the world's most valuable artworks. Rare rocks and stones were placed each on its own dais or hanging by cords from the ceiling. No mirrors, no clocks. A fountain of pure soft light at the middle of the vast space gave forth a pleasing sound.

The guests were greeting each other, melodious, friendly. In here, she thought, you could meet those you'd known in another reality. They were warm, with light energy. Evolved, she decided. These were beautiful spirits only looking like people. The scent of flowers and herbs was enough pleasure. Huge whirls of colourful smoke lifted, obedient to the high vast ceiling, and curled through an aperture out into the night. 'These are spirits having a human experience.'

'I'm talking to myself,' she said aloud. 'I am drugged. This is a dream.'

A group assembled on their way to look at the gardens. 'Come with us,' they invited her. The band played an old fifties ballad. 'Why this music?' a woman asked her partner.

'Because He likes it.' The 'He' was emphasized.

A man in evening suit with quite long distinguished white hair pushed open a door and he stopped and turned and it was as though he 'saw her'. He made a sign to the band and they stopped and played *Smoke Gets in Your Eyes*.

'How strange,' she said. 'I haven't heard that for years. Not since I first came to Spain a long time ago. It was the music Sal Roca and I danced to.' She shivered. He was here. And she knew it. And she tried to make her way through the group which continually wound one way and another denying her entrance.

She did not see him. They passed each other. They never spoke. She did not recognize him. They never met.

On the way down she told Gerard they were not people. They were spirits. They only looked like people. They are not from here.

He can't hear you. You can't bring anything back from Paradise.

And she had seen the man with the beautiful lustrous white hair arrive in front of her as she was leaving the auditorium. He walked sideways in front of her as though in a dance, dropping rose petals along her path.

'I've been drugged,' she said as Gerard lifted her from the car. 'It's beautiful up there but it doesn't exist. Beautiful isn't enough of a word to describe but I don't have another. Not down here.'

It's more real than what any drug can give you. Just remember you've been there. In your worst and best moments that place is there for you.

The next morning Mercedes came to the hotel and said immediately Mia looked different. 'You went up to The Rich on the Hill last night.'

'It was. . . .' She was going to say, 'extraordinary'. But it was more. 'It has its own reality. I think they put something in the entrance drink.'

Mercedes waited for her to say more.

'It sounds as though something magical happened there.'

Again, Mercedes waited.

'How does it exist? Who owns it?' Mia asked.

'Paradise?' said Mercedes. 'He does.'

'Sal Roca?'

So, she hadn't seen him. Mercedes had put a lot of effort into that chance meeting.

'He wasn't there,' said Mia.

As her mother used to say, 'the penny dropped' and she rushed around to the gym before Mercedes went off for lunch.

'Did he know I was coming?'

'No,' said Mercedes.

They hadn't recognized each other. Mercedes could see that.

Mia said, 'He wasn't there.' And then she remembered only too well the man with the white hair and the rose petals. '*Smoke Gets in Your Eyes*. We used to dance to that.'

'He wants you to have this,' and Mercedes gave her the envelope.

'How does he know I'm here?'

Mercedes had told him the reason Mia was here. The illness, the love. The envelope was his way of showing gratitude for their past.

The envelope had the details they all searched for. Where it was. The way to reach it. The note was simple. 'I give you this. For all that we found together.'

Before she left for Mt O she went back again to Mercedes. 'The message was wonderful. At first. But it didn't say he would see me.' She had kept the envelope away from the others. She simply said she had been given verbally precise directions. What was it about human beings they had to cling to their valuables, their secrets?

'Can I see him?' she asked Mercedes.

For a moment Mercedes wanted to toss the problem to Gerard but she cared enough for Mia to take the passing on of the revelation herself. 'You remember I said the other day money had come to town and there were people I didn't see anymore? Too up the ladder for me. You are part of this town because you helped him with the uncovering of Cabala and you were at the beginning of the Arc Bar. You were a free spirit and people appreciated that. So, you deserve to be recognized for that. Gerard didn't remember. He's too young. A Chinese visited shortly after the Cabala centre opened. And she came back.'

'She'. Mia knew now how this was going to unfold and she sat on the nearest seat.

The Chinese certainly put money into the restoration of the Cabala centre. Then she was gone, supposedly for years. Then she came back here from New York and decided to live here. She literally bought a village in the countryside. And then uncovered things about Mt O and became interested, and bankrolled the place. For him. Sal Roca is her partner in all these acquisitions. She is obviously super wealthy and has a group around her. She's a direct descendant of Empress Wu of the Tang dynasty, seventh century.

'She probably bought that too,' said Mia. 'The lineage.'

Mercedes laughed. It was easier than she thought. 'And she's possessive. Of him. Always has been. So, Gerard, through connections, made it possible for you to enter that place. Sal Roca is always there so chances are you would see each other.' She paused. 'So afterwards I called Sal Roca and told him you'd been there. And you know what? He thought he had seen someone that looked like you. He had thought about you all that night. I told him your story. He said he'd think about it. He rang back and said he would have an envelope delivered. His gift to you.'

'But we don't get to meet.'

'But you get something else. You get to climb a low mountain. It's only a couple of hours up there.'

'Can you tell him I'm going up?' She made a decision. 'This evening.'

Mercedes became safe and straight-faced. 'I got the feeling the envelope was as much as he could do. But I'll try.' She hugged her.

'What's she like? The partner?'

'Extraordinarily turned out. Out of this world. She doesn't come down here. Not since she's opened that place. She's always up there or in a helicopter off to some airport.'

'Does she know he's given me the information?'

'I doubt it. She's too busy looking at Venus.'

The grey woman, as she became known, was still there but would not resonate with anything. 'I'm ordinary. I don't do anything exciting.'

The workshop group couldn't stand her. Mia saw it as a spiritual failure on her part and tried to talk her out of leaving. 'You've got an amazing wonderful spirit and you can do unique things that are just for you.'

'What things?'

'I'm sure we'll find out.'

The woman had arrived two days ago and Cynthia had encouraged her to join the group. It wasn't clear whether she was a tourist in the wrong place.

Belle had worked out the Grail exercise that morning, 'We work as normal and slip away when they least expect it. Use the grey woman as an excuse to just finally walk away.'

The woman was grey in appearance and character but not without opinions. 'This is not my sort of thing. To be honest I'm from the north and we don't do these sorts of things. I don't like these sorts of people. Stuck up.'

180

Cynthia, to keep her at least for the next hour said, 'Well, just stay around and give it another day.'

It got worse and ended with Lily sitting on the wall crying. 'This isn't what I'm here for.' The woman said she would like to speak in private to Mia. They went for a walk along the old wall of the city. The woman said, 'I like you. I can see you've been through it. But you're honest. Also, I want my money back.'

Oh shit! thought Mia. She would. There was no money. She asked the woman what she did.

'The same as us normal people like you and me.'

Chance would be a fine thing, Mia.

'It's not only the people. It's something about this place,' the woman said.

'Yes,' said Mia. 'It brings out things in us that normally we don't feel. But it makes us deeper and richer. What is your name?'

'I've already told you twice.'

Mia asked what she did up north.

'I don't live there now. I came from there.' Mia thought, I bet she comes from somewhere truly awful like—she couldn't think of anywhere bad enough. Like Milton Keynes. She asked her where she lived now. Please don't say Milton Keynes.

'Croydon.'

'Why are you here?'

'I had a kid who had a daughter. She was very beautiful. I used to go and wait for her to come out of school. I never spoke to her. But she had something that brightened my life. And then I heard that she'd become famous. It didn't surprise me. Then I heard she was here.'

Mia, icy cold, didn't need to know the name.

'I saved up all my money to come here. I'm just her grandmother.'

That made her the fourth grandmother. But according to the skull there would be only three claiming the Grail. Who would drop out?

Chapter 23

Belle packed the water, food, boots, rain jackets and a torch. She said, 'It's probable The Cat has set her grandmother up to see what we've found. A family member on the prowl—too much! Gerard has got Vicky Smart a talk at the Culture Centre. Best thing that could happen. They're all going and we go up the mountain. She's good. Presents well.'

'Too clever for me,' said Cynthia. 'And what is a chemical wedding? Aren't they all chemical? She's no grandmother.'

Cynthia was still lying flat and resistant. Belle teased her foot. 'Not sure. So that's why we're going up there right now. And first. And why Gerard is taking us to the start point in the car. If we roll out with this luggage, they'll spot it. Eric will be disguised as a wolf quicker than he's combed that hair to see where we're going.'

'I just wanted one more day,' said Cynthia.

'Why?'

'In case I don't come back.'

Cynthia, no one likes change.

To get to the car they had to pass through crowds of people dressed in old-fashioned clothes carrying weapons and scrolls.

'It's for the pageant,' Gerard said. 'Every year they have a replay of the nineteenth-century war with the French. They run all over the countryside catching mock enemies.' The participants were noisy and some more than a little drunk.

Gerard drove as close to the start point as he could. Mia repeated the verbal instructions she had been given. She still did not trust anyone enough to show the drawing Sal Roca had sent or the other contents in the envelope.

'Remember, stay on the left side away from the wind,' said Gerard. 'And my mobile is on.' He leaned forward close to Belle and took both her hands gently, placed them together, and enclosed them inside his. He looked into her eyes wishing the best for her. With one hand he took the chain with its cross from around his neck and put it around hers. Then he got their bags out of the car. 'I'll stay close.'

Belle said before they started the ascent they should stand together and get honest. 'I will start. I know where I will go to be free, where I really belong. Back to the old summerhouse of my childhood at the end of the fjord. They will never find me there. Sometimes I long for the smell of the moss in summer.'

Cynthia standing next to her, looking up at Mt O, said she didn't want the Grail and where could she put it? On her mantlepiece?

Mia said, 'My son from the rock-star was an addict too. I gave him a lot of my money. People say I am an enabler. It killed him eventually. His child, my granddaughter, had a terrible life and I did everything I could, spent every buck on rehab. People said I was co-dependent. I ended broke. I'm certainly not co-dependent on life.'

They started up but from the bottom, could not see the top. 'It could be a long way,' said Belle. 'Forget hill. Small mountain.'

To get their minds off the climbing they talked about getting older. Cynthia said she had to have more bladder awareness. Mia mentioned forgetfulness.

Belle led the way.

'What do we do with it?' said Cynthia already out of breath.' How big is it?'

That made Belle pause and she called a tea stop and got out the thermos. It was the Blue Hour but from this place there was no view. Belle was listening and could hear sounds she did not like. She stood up. 'Come on, grandmothers. Let's get to it before dark. Gerard said it will take a good hour.'

They climbed and walked and had to help each other over rocks, small ravines, pools of mud which took over two hours. Cynthia, seriously tired, had to take a rest. Mia's bones ached and she used a method she had found on the first day of the tour and concentrated her thoughts on the exterior so not registering the interior pain.

'I can't go much further,' Cynthia said.

Then they heard the gunshots.

'Oh shit!' said Belle. 'Lie flat.'

They couldn't tell how far away they were or from what direction. 'They're certainly not killing rabbits,' said Belle. 'My moneys on The Cat.'

Terrified now, Mia produced Sal Roca's map.

'We can't use a torch,' said Belle. 'Or we will give away our position.' She gave Cynthia a shot of brandy and pulled her further up a new set of rocky hell. 'We can't speak from now on. Whisper.' More gunfire seemingly from all sides. From behind a tree Belle called Gerard.

'It's not the security,' he said. He heard the shots. 'It sounds like blanks from the rifle musket fire. It's the guys in the pageant.'

Around another slope. Here the caves should begin. Belle got out the torch and read the map. 'Further up. Just breathe and climb.' Cynthia said she could not.

'If you get up here your next year will be lighter and braver,' said Belle. 'You will have done something marvellous. Come on.' She pulled Cynthia and Mia pushed. The noise of their ascent alerted the animals. Gunfire nearer, men shouting. Mia ducked to avoid a possible bullet. Helicopter in the distance coming closer. 'Now we pray,' said Belle. 'Crawl,' she said, 'and leave our bags behind this rock. They're trying to scare us back down.'

'I don't trust Gerard,' said Cynthia.

'Maybe blanks but sounds more like gunfire to me,' said Belle.

They did find the first cave. Mia had gone beyond pain, Cynthia was stung by insects, heart out of rhythm, blinded with heat. Mia and Belle carried her up the last slope, into the cave. Was it here?

'I can't risk light.' Even Belle was exhausted. Cynthia was not in a good way.

'Let's just ask for help,' said Mia.

Cynthia shook her head. Sound of feet speeding past the cave.

'Did you tell anyone else?' Belle asked. She lit a match. And there it was. The stone cup. It rested just easy against the wall of the cave. They were all breathless, silent, shocked. Slowly, one by one they approached the stone. It made Mia feel better.

This wondrous object propped up against the cave wall amounted to so little, it could be anything. All thought, all fear ceased as they looked at the stone vessel. And then Mia tried to lift it and it was heavy even with Belle's assistance. 'What is it made of? Nothing I've seen,' said Mia. 'The stone around here is mostly granite.'

The other oddness was the shape. The cup was tall as though stretching upwards. 'For a moment it looked alive,' said Mia.

'It's definitely moved,' said Belle. 'It was more to one side when we came in.'

Mia was now too nervous to touch it. 'Please don't move,' she said to the cup. 'I can't take it. Now it's taller than me.'

Belle shone the torch deeper to the ground. 'It's on a kind of pedestal. It's attached to it.' She touched the stand and pulled her hand away fast. 'It's hot.' Then the torch flickered and jumped out of her hand.

Mia tapped the light on her phone and gave it to Belle. 'Maybe it has come from a vast distance through space and hasn't cooled down yet. I think we should give it some reverence or respect. We can't just be in here with this magnificent channel of light and other life.' Mia tried to make out its colour.

They realized Cynthia wasn't talking. She was too overwrought for speech. Breathing was her problem. The cave smelt of herbs with an underlying trace of mould.

'We will go down slowly,' said Belle.

''How do we carry it?' said Mia.

'How do we carry me?' said Cynthia.

They crouched by the stone cup, quiet, not moving. Mia whispered, 'I have the feeling it's alive.'

Belle said, 'There's all that rumpus outside and we haven't even heard it. It's as though we are somewhere else.' Belle's hand went towards the cup again. 'There's too much velocity. A piece of a star? How do we get it down?'

'It doesn't want to be taken,' said Mia. And as though from nowhere she added, 'That's all human beings can do. Photograph it, hide it, try and own it.'

'I have not come through all this to hear that,' said Cynthia suddenly. 'It's ours.'

Her claim seemed out of date suddenly.

185

'One of us has to go for help,' said Belle. 'I'll stay here with Cynthia and Mia goes and gets Gerard.' She had seen the swelling on Cynthia's foot and hoped it was just a bite but not a snake bite.

'Gerard and his guys can take Cynthia down. I'll stay with the Grail,' said Mia. 'Phone him now to meet us.'

'I'll not leave it and that's that,' said Cynthia angry.

'OK,' said Belle. 'Mia and I will take you down and meet Gerard and he'll take you down further in the car. And then I'll come back.'

'Never!' said Cynthia.

'I get the idea you don't trust me,' said Belle.

'We'll all stay together here in the cave. Why should I be tossed out of here by your lover?' said Cynthia.

The row that followed rivalled the war re-enactment playing outside. It shocked them all and they were suddenly silent.

'I'll go upwards and get help from Paradise,' said Mia. 'I can get to Sal Roca. He can get his guards to carry it to a car or into a helicopter and...'

'Never!' said Cynthia.

'Then we're all stuck,' said Belle. 'We'll just perish up here.'

'I hardly know you,' Cynthia told her. 'You could take this priceless cup and never be seen again.'

The row that followed was worse. Could this be the three inmates of the Decision Chamber getting ready to claim a mountain in high spiritual mood? And now they disliked each other to the point of breaking their friendship because of an object they couldn't even carry.

'The main problem is Gerard.' Cynthia was convinced Belle would persuade him to get his men and remove the object while Mia went up to get help from Paradise.

Mia was upset, almost crying. 'What do we actually do with it? Cut it in three?'

'Sell it,' said Belle. 'There's plenty of sky-high offers out there. We take it to a mutual place and put out the info and wait for the bids.'

'And we stay together,' said Cynthia.

'Certainly,' said Belle frostily. 'I'll come and live with you.'

186

'Ed could come and get it in a car,' said Cynthia. 'He knows about these things,'

'Look, it's the greatest thing on this planet. You can't take it to your home,' said Belle.

'I'd feel better about it,' said Cynthia.

'I bet you would!'

And suddenly they stopped.

'I don't believe this has happened,' said Mia, face stained with tears. Even the Grail Cup looked as though it had collapsed sideways.

Mia went back to look at it again. 'It can't have moved. It must be the way the light changed.'

'Together we might be able to lift it,' said Belle softly, regaining respect. 'But we would never get it down the hill of Mt O.'

They stayed silent and exhausted.

For a short while they had hated each other. At one point Mia didn't care if she was shot.

'But we love each other,' said Cynthia feebly. 'We can't do this.'

'We have found something so valuable and incredible. And what happens? We hate each other.' Mia couldn't look at her. 'After all it was my lover who ... gave it to me.'

'We have to leave it,' said Belle. 'It's brought out the worst in us.'

'But all we got was a glimpse,' said Cynthia.

'Maybe that's all we get,' said Mia. 'Of anything in life.'

Cynthia said they must hide it. 'We can't just leave it.'

'Why not?' said Mia.

'The others will find it. Gerard has his price,' said Cynthia.

Belle, afraid, reacted and suggested they hide it behind rocks in the cave.

'Whatever for?' said Mia.' We can't carry it and parts of it are too hot. Leave it where it is. I have a feeling it can look after itself.' And if it couldn't Sal Roca would. Of that she was sure.

'It is serene.' Belle made a slight, private, almost reverent, gesture to this almost friendly stone.

'What we discovered for each other — more wonderful than trying to own it,' said Cynthia.

And from the stone came a sound, almost a reverberation that Mia said afterwards was 'like gold'. Even the gunfire and rush of soldiers, mock or otherwise, had ceased.

The going down was easier and lighter. They discussed the stone's sound. Was it ticking? Belle thought it was alive. And then they recognized their love for each other had come first and before anything.

And the grandmothers agreed that in this they had found the Holy Grail.

Books to challenge your perception of reality

A message from Clairview

We are an independent publishing company with a focus on cutting-edge, non-fiction books. Our innovative list covers current affairs and politics, health, the arts, history, science and spirituality. But regardless of subject, our books have a common link: they all question conventional thinking, dogmas and received wisdom.

Despite being a small company, our list features some big names, such as Booker Prize winner Ben Okri, literary giant Gore Vidal, world leader Mikhail Gorbachev, modern artist Joseph Beuys and natural childbirth pioneer Michel Odent.

So, check out our full catalogue online at
www.clairviewbooks.com
and join our emailing list for news on new titles.

office@clairviewbooks.com

CLAIRVIEW